The Shotgun Wedding

The Shotgun Wedding

a novel

Suchandra Roychowdhury

ALEPH

ALEPH BOOK COMPANY
An independent publishing firm
promoted by *Rupa Publications India*

First published in India in 2022
by Aleph Book Company
7/16 Ansari Road, Daryaganj
New Delhi 110 002

ISBN: 978-93-91047-21-4

1 3 5 7 9 10 8 6 4 2

Printed at Thomson Press India Ltd., Faridabad

In memory of my father,
Sri Subrata Dasgupta

Contents

Prologue

Sunshine penetrated into his soul, stinging and stabbing, burning and bruising. Bhuwan squeezed his eyes shut, his nut-brown, weather-beaten face resigned to fate and fatigue as he raised his head to the remorseless brilliance of a cloudless sky. The rain gods have been elusive this year, he sighed. Wiping the beads of perspiration off his forehead with a frayed piece of cloth, he sat down amidst the stalks of ripened corn undulating like a wave of gold in the breeze, relaxing for a fleeting instant before going back to the toil and trouble of life lived at subsistence level.

'Bhuwan,' a strident voice cut across the field, 'Bhuwan!' The voice rippled over the amber stalks, reverberating in the stillness that hovered over a parched season and days bleached white by the sun. Bhuwan stood up slowly, his frail form trembling at the unexpected intrusion. Even from a distance he could make out Vishnu running towards him, waving desperately to grab his attention. Clearly out of breath as he approached Bhuwan, Vishnu still managed to blurt out his momentous news. 'Don't you know what's happening?' he gasped. 'At long last, change is coming to Phulpukur.'

Bhuwan could not comprehend why Vishnu was so thrilled; in all the years that he had lived there, nothing exciting had ever happened in Phulpukur. Bhuwan's eyes clouded with incomprehension; Bhuwan was sure of one thing—nothing could or would change. Phulpukur was eternal and so was the despondency that eclipsed the lives of tenant farmers like Vishnu and him. So why all the euphoria? After all, no one in the outside world was bothered about Phulpukur.

Tucked away in the southernmost corner of West Bengal, in the marine delta zone of South 24 Parganas district, Phulpukur was a sleepy little village, whose existence, unfortunately, was inconsequential to the rest of the world. Once upon a time, however, the district had been the capital of Maharaja Pratapaditya of Jessore, who challenged the mighty Mughal empire and established the independence of southern Bengal. Not much of that glorious past had survived, eroded by time and a general disregard of history, as successive generations of Phulpukur's inhabitants had been transformed into a breed of stoic humanity, struggling to meet the bare necessities of life.

In the not so recent past, Phulpukur and its surrounding district used to be an extension of mangrove forests and saltwater swamps that formed a part of the Ganges delta. The terrain—marshy, damp, and dank—was virtually uninhabited; only a handful of farmers like Bhuwan and Vishnu struggled to cultivate small patches of arable land, breaking their backs to yield a pitiable harvest of rice, sugarcane, timber, and betel nut.

Summer in Phulpukur could be unbearable, the heat and dust choking the lifeblood out of the farmers. The sun drenched the rural landscape in layers of heat, saturating the farms and the waterbodies with such sparkling brilliance that the simmering greens and blues of the land seemed on the verge of vaporizing into the turquoise of the sky. Hot and humid air hung like a pall over the paddy fields, as sunburnt farmers went about their work, following the standard practice of planting seeds and cultivating crops day after day, year after year with rigorous monotony. It was an exhausting routine, and a dull, hard, unimaginative life, but no one was really complaining.

Despite the hardship, the spirit that echoes in the air of Phulpukur resonates with an intrinsic sense of pride and love that has no monetary value. Bhuwan and Vishnu, their sons Rajeev and Utpal, and most of the tenant farmers like them, lived in thatched rickety shanties, with open verandas covered with tarpaulin. During the monsoon, Rajeev and Utpal would bemoan the fact that their humble home would be engulfed in mud and slush and grime, but they had learned to live with it. Their kitchens were clay ovens built in the darkness of the common passage between two houses. These tumbledown huts often housed large families and whenever the occupants needed privacy, they would set up partitions between their rooms with old saris. The flexible jugaad psyche, so very quintessential to India, abounded in this village.

Pockets of affluence in Phulpukur were few and far between, but they were there nonetheless: a sprinkling of landowners; a few descendants of an infamous dacoit who had roamed the land decades earlier and had left a handsome fortune for his heirs to enjoy; and a couple of families associated with a somewhat dilapidated missionary organization, Saint James Mission School, which had initially sought to proselytize and educate but had given up all hopes of converting people to Christianity a long time ago, although it continued its existence as a desultory educational institute, crumbling with age and history.

And then, in 2006, Phulpukur reached the nadir of its existence: the Indian Ministry of Panchayati Raj declared South 24 Parganas as one of the country's most backward districts and Phulpukur as a penurious village. Finally waking up to the miserable plight of the people residing in this part of the world, it was unanimously agreed in the hallowed corridors of the Indian parliament that the western side of the district was to be designated as a special economic zone, with the focus on promoting agriculture, industry, and pisciculture. But first, the populace needed to be educated to meet the challenges of civilization and progress. How else can you manipulate an unlettered and unenlightened and, therefore, unresponsive and uncomprehending mind?

This decision, taken from on high, led to an ironic set of situations. When people are not actually planning for a better future, or looking for any significant change, someone else has to do it for them; in Phulpukur's case, the intrusion into its less than idyllic existence came in the guise of a literacy drive by the government. Phulpukurians watched with unabashed wonder as schools, and then, this particular summer, a college opened its gates in an effort to bring enlightenment to the average villager's mind.

Students from the neighbouring vidhan sabha constituencies of Gosaba, Basanti, Kultali, and Mandirbazar started trickling into Phulpukur, thus adding to the substantial body of local youngsters who sought enrolment in the college. Education brought in its wake a vicious cycle of politics. Bhuwan, Vishnu, and many other hapless farmers were left to deal with their cultivation on their own as their sons and daughters, armed with books and political manifestos, joined the fray of belligerent youths to usher in development. From then on, life in Phulpukur was never the same again.

This metamorphosis, when it reached Phulpukur, had far-reaching effects, notable among which was the appointment of Dita Roy in the post of full-time lecturer in Phulpukur College. This unsuspecting lady, sans any previous exposure to politics in rural Bengal, managed to land herself in the eye of the storm that was brewing over the village and was inextricably linked to the scandal that gained perpetual notoriety in West Bengal as the Shotgun Wedding.

The story—featuring stratagems worthy of a chess grandmaster, played out by flawed protagonists, wily politicians with their mafioso contacts, and damsels in distress—captured the national consciousness. Although the headline grabbing events put Phulpukur on the national map, the story began on an unremarkable note....

Being and Nothingness

*R*ed dust swirled around the dirt track, and a veil of sand particles rose from the parched earth to envelop a small white car bumping along the uneven surface of the makeshift road, gingerly avoiding potholes before coming to a somewhat unsure halt in front of an old and crumbling brick wall. A window rolled down and a rather anxious face looked out, trying to figure out the lay of the land.

Behind the brick wall, two sets of eyes peered out with avid interest from a window on the third floor of the ancient school building to take stock of the intruder in the white car. The driver seemed to be undecided whether to step out or not, but the two men on the third floor leaned out even further to catch their first glimpse of the occupant of the car.

'Don't fling yourself right out of the window, Gopal,' Raja reprimanded his over-eager companion. 'You won't get a better view if you fly out like a jaybird.'

'Look who's talking,' Gopal grumbled as he stepped back. 'You shouldn't even be here today, considering the fact that the person in the car will create quite a ripple here in the village and your father won't like it if you strike up an acquaintance even before he arrives on the scene.'

Raja's gaze shifted from the motionless car and noted the look of apprehension that clouded Gopal's usually cheerful countenance. Lines of anxiety made deep furrows on Gopal's forehead as the overweight, middle-aged man tried to warn Raja of the consequences of trying to outshine his father. 'Go away,' Gopal urged, wringing his pudgy hands in desperation, tugging at the rumpled sleeve of Raja's once-white shirt.

'No way, I'm not budging. Why should Palash Bose have the upper hand in everything that happens around here?' Raja grinned wickedly. 'Let's upstage him for once.'

Eyes shining with devilish merriment, Raja continued leaning out of the window. In the twenty-four years of his life, people around him often remarked on the striking quality of his alert grey eyes beneath dark crescent-shaped eyebrows. His face was arresting, prominent cheekbones and a strong jaw belying the curious vulnerability of youth, and there was a hint of arrogance in the way he sometimes looked down his aquiline nose from his height of six feet two inches. An ever-present spark of mischief added to his raffish charm.

A few errant strands of jet-black hair blurred Raja's vision as he looked down, having to bend almost double to fit his tall frame into that of the window. He was finally rewarded by the sight of the driver timidly stepping out of the car, obviously intimidated by the imposing relic from the days of the Raj that confronted her. The school building was indeed a fascinating piece of architecture and rather imposing.

'Gopal, you won't believe this,' Raja whispered, an undercurrent of laughter lacing his words. Gopal rushed back to the window, just in time to catch a glimpse of the frail young woman, dressed in a blue salwar kameez who emerged from the car. Her wispy chiffon dupatta unfurled like a butterfly in the wind, all aflutter with curiosity, until she gathered it back with an impatient tug. Her small and delicate face had an elfin charm, especially when lit up with a mischievous smile. The smile, however, was absent at this moment, a dense shadow of uncertainty obscuring the usual cheerfulness of her expressive dark eyes. She looked around warily: it was all terra incognita to her—vast, incomprehensible, and unknown.

'Raja, your father will be far from pleased,' Gopal whispered, apprehensive and hesitant. 'He certainly wasn't expecting a woman for the post which has opened up in the college.'

'No, the old fox won't like it at all,' Raja agreed. 'I thought he mentioned someone named Aditya Roy who was being sent by the College Service Commission. It's not often that he gets things wrong...' he broke off as he made eye contact with the lady in question.

Dita looked up, craning her neck and squinting against the rays of a merciless sun, as she spotted the two figures on the third floor. From ground level, they appeared like two curious marionettes attached by tenuous strings to a lopsided windowpane. They were the only people around in the imposing but crumbling structure in front of her, and were leaning so far out of the window that she was immediately concerned for their safety. From her position of evident disadvantage, she could just about make out that, of the two, one was obviously younger. She hesitated for a moment and then beckoned him to come down.

Raja gave an infinitesimal nod of understanding, indicating that he was heading downstairs.

'Don't forget to take the keys,' Gopal instructed. 'It's

still early, the school gates haven't been opened yet. And don't you think that you should first change out of the clothes that you are wearing? They are at least two sizes too big for you. I only gave them to you last night to sleep in them, not to make a public appearance in them,' Gopal remonstrated. 'Your father will have my hide if he sees you like this.'

Raja shrugged, remembering the altercation that he had had with his father the night before—another clash of wills and ideals in an interminable series of disagreements—following which he had walked out in a fit of pique. Way too rattled to go back home for the night, he had sought out Gopal in the Saint James Mission School canteen, shared his food, changed into his oversized clothes, and fallen into a dreamless sleep. Which was why, early this morning, Raja was still lounging in Gopal's kitchen, looking rather scruffy, when they heard the car come to a halt in front of the school gates. He ignored Gopal's protestations; displeasing his father seemed to have a charm of its own. A ghost of a smile hovered on his lips as he picked up the keys and headed out of the room. A few notes of 'Wind of Change' by Scorpions floated unbidden into his mind; almost unconsciously he started whistling the tune as he ran down the stairs.

His jaunty mood was somewhat shaken as he approached the school's tall and rusty iron gates, worn and ancient and covered with shrubs. He stopped short, sensing the waves of tension oozing out of the slight figure looking at him with apprehensive eyes from the other side of the antiquated portal. She was delicate and petite and pale with anxiety. Raja found himself peering down at her yet again. Her eyes widened in shock as he approached; he sighed as he realized the impression he must be making right now, grimy and slouchy in borrowed clothes. She would surely take him for a vagrant of some sort.

Gopal, who was still leaning out of the third-floor window flailing his plump arms like an ineffective octopus, tried to ease the awkward situation. 'Take her to the principal's office, the doors are open and she can wait there till the office staff come in,' and then added as an afterthought, 'meanwhile you can come up and get her some tea.' In Gopal's universe, tea was the panacea for every conceivable problem.

The gates creaked open as Raja pushed back one side of the imposing barrier, and the anxious woman stepped in. 'I'm sorry, but I was looking for Phulpukur College, and the villagers pointed me in this direction,' she cast a troubled glance at Raja, far from reassured by his dishevelled appearance. 'But I see this is a school campus, not a college?'

Raja chose not to answer the question immediately, instead choosing to ask a question of his own. 'Have you been appointed by the College Service Commission to take up a post in Phulpukur College?'

'Yes,' came the startled reply; she was surprised that he knew so much.

'You've come to the right place then,' Raja tried to reassure her, as he ushered her through the colonial arches towards the principal's office. 'Phulpukur College is still in its nascent stage, and because it does not have an independent campus of its own, classes are conducted here, on the second floor of Saint James School.'

Dita tried to keep her panic in check. No campus?

What exactly did this unkempt stranger mean? She tried to keep pace with him, all but breaking into a run as he loped ahead with long-legged strides. Sensing that she was having trouble keeping up with him, Raja paused, turning around and pinning her down with his startling grey eyes. 'The members of the governing body are trying their best to mobilize the college campus, which is coming up on a stretch of land further down the road,' he informed her, taking in the shock reflected on her face with deep sympathy. It was not a promising situation, and she had not even met his father, Palash Bose, who was the president of the governing body of Phulpukur College. Palash would be an unsurmountable challenge that she would obviously have to deal with.

Raja opened the doors to the principal's office and escorted her in, gesturing towards one of the time-worn leather chairs for her to sit in and wait. She looked dazed as she took in the outdated furniture, the gloom of the chamber broken by stray beams of sunlight creeping through the transom windows. Books and journals, mouldy with age, lined the shelves running across the walls. Speechless and uneasy, Dita sat down.

Everything about this place was intriguing, a village school with echoes from the colonial past, a room lined with journals which seemed to have antiquarian value, a ragamuffin with a clipped, polished accent and sophisticated vocabulary; and could it be her imagination, or was he actually whistling 'Wind of Change'? Strange indeed!

Raja could see the anxiety warring with curiosity on her face and tried to ease it somewhat by giving her a brief background of the place. 'This school was built by Christian missionaries, labouring under the white man's burden to preach, proselytize, and educate,' he chuckled. 'Fortunately for Phulpukur, the edifice they built survived the Raj. Though it's a bit dilapidated and maintained on a severely constricted cash flow, it's still impressive.'

His words were rudely interrupted by Gopal calling out to Raja from upstairs. Raja rushed out, offering an impish grin as he left. 'I'll be back with some tea for you. I guess you could use a cup before you meet the governing body of the college.'

Almost half an hour later, when the young man still hadn't appeared with that promised cup of tea, the doors to the principal's office opened again and a small crowd stepped in. A tall and imposing figure led the group, dressed in a pristine white dhoti and kurta, gold-rimmed glasses sitting on the bridge of an aquiline nose, shrewd eyes glinting behind the lenses as he took in the slight figure who looked back at him anxiously.

His hands went up in the traditional Bengali greeting, 'Namoshkar, I am Palash Bose, president of the governing body, Phulpukur College. I retired from the post of principal of Diamond Harbour College two years ago and since then it has been my mission to work for this college.' The crowd behind stood in near obsequious silence as he continued, 'So sorry to keep you waiting, we came as soon as we received news about your arrival from Gopal. Though I must confess, I was expecting someone named Aditya Roy?' he gave her a quizzical look, silently challenging her as if she were an impostor.

'The College Service Commission is not infallible, I guess; they must have made a mess of my name,' she drew out a document from her voluminous handbag and handed it over to Palash Bose. 'This is my appointment letter. I am Dita Roy; I will be taking up the post of lecturer in the English Department of Phulpukur College.'

The crowd shuffled its feet and someone at the rear tittered, 'English Department in Phulpukur? Whoever heard of that?'

Palash turned around, his displeasure evident on his face. The crowd fell silent once again. Having gained control over the crowd, he fixed his attention on the hapless newcomer. 'Dita, that's an unusual name, no wonder they made a hash of it. If I remember correctly, it's the name of the medicinal bark of the *Alstonia scholaris*, an East Asian tree.'

Dita was impressed: the man was knowledgeable, to say the least, and obviously in control of the people surrounding him. Following his lead, they all settled down around an immense mahogany table and Palash began introducing Dita to the members of the governing body.

'This is Salim Khan, my deputy, he looks after the financial matters of the college. He will be more than willing to help you with your maths, if you so require.' Salim wobbled his head from side to side to indicate his acquiescence. 'And this is Mukul Nath, my right-hand man and jack of all trades,' Palash continued, indicating the lanky person on his left, a bag of skin and bones with bulging eyes.

Noticing that nearly all of them were clad in pristine white dhotis and kurtas, which contrasted sharply with their dark skins, Dita had the eerie feeling that she was caught in the frames of a black-and-white movie or possibly a film noir. She had never seen so many dhoti-clad men together in one place, except perhaps at fancy Bong weddings. Grouped together in their white attire, they bore an absurd resemblance to the chorus of classical Greek theatre, obeying the dictates of the chorus leader, Palash Bose.

Dita felt uneasy and distinctly out of place as the only woman in a bizarre and clearly unexpected setting, bearing the scrutiny of an all-male gaze. She shook herself mentally— this was not the moment to be cowed down. A gleam of steel entered her eyes. 'Just so you know, I have been appointed by the College Service Commission as a lecturer of English; maths is not my area of interest or expertise. Why would I need help with maths?'

Dita could not help but notice that Palash Bose's smile did not reach his eyes, which reflected his sharp intelligence, keenness, and shrewdness, but were curiously devoid of warmth.

'Your job description might not entirely be pigeonholed to teaching English classes. There are so many things you will have to do here. You'll need to plan for the college building first, won't you? And that will entail layers and layers of financial accounting, won't it?' Palash retorted.

Dita shivered as waves of incomprehensible foreboding made her go numb; what was she being dragged into?

'Since you are the first government appointee to this college, you have to become the provisional principal.' He let the surprise sink in slowly. 'You are the captain of this ship now,' he said with a frown, loathe to hand over the reins to an obviously inexperienced woman, a greenhorn.

It was a punch in the solar plexus for Dita. Not even in her wildest dreams had she imagined that she would be facing such an unusual situation. Besides, she had had no prior exposure whatsoever to the administrative side of running an educational institute. She glanced helplessly at the curious faces looking down at her, judging her, dismissing her as a city girl incapable of handling the challenges of a campus in a village. She won't last a day, seemed to be the silent consensus behind the poker faces.

Ignoring her bewilderment, Palash continued with the introductions. Turning to a rather elegant-looking man dressed in a richly embroidered red kurta and spotless white dhoti, he said, 'This is Aditya Pundit, you can say he has been single-handedly responsible for setting up the college here in Phulpukur.' Indicating the two identical-looking young men by his side, he added, 'These are Aditya's sons, Papu and Pinku; as you can see, they are identical twins. It is often very difficult to tell them apart,' he almost smiled.

'They have been of great help in organizing the administrative side of the college. It was Aditya's father Durjoy Pundit's dream to bring higher education to the village, and over three generations the Pundit family has dedicated itself to this task.'

By this time, Palash had warmed to his role as the chorus leader. 'The Pundits were local zamindars, who had fallen on hard times soon after India won her Independence. Durjoy turned out to be the black sheep of his family. Unlike the other heirs and descendants, he had no interest in getting himself educated. Instead of books, he picked up guns and became one of the most notorious dacoits of this area. Legend has it that he amassed a hefty fortune, and since he led a Spartan lifestyle, he hardly spent any of it. He must have regretted the error of his ways, because in the last few years of his life he longed for the one thing he never had—education. On his deathbed, he instructed his sons to open a college in his name, here, in the village of Phulpukur.

'It was easier said than done,' said Palash, 'Durjoy's sons

approached the Ministry of Education, who were obviously not inclined to set up a college in memory of an infamous criminal. Fortunately, a compromise was reached.... Durjoy's sons donated land for the college as well as a handsome amount of money to start off the construction. But the college would not be named after Durjoy, it would simply be known as Phulpukur College. A marble plaque would be installed on the premises in Durjoy's name and a life-size portrait of him would be put up in the hall of fame.'

Here, Palash stopped, looking inexplicably sad. Pinku picked up the narrative. 'All the plans were in place.... But then something unexpected happened.' He paused dramatically. 'State elections! And Raktokarobi, the party which had ruled unchallenged for the last decade, fell flat on its face. Everything went haywire and Shyamol Sathi, hitherto a fledgling party at best, waltzed into power. Caught in the web of transition, the fate of the college dangled in bureaucratic limbo for years and years.'

'It came as a surprise to us all, when it was finally approved,' Papu broke in. 'But the funds were yet to be released for the building. The headmaster of Saint James floated the idea that we could start off with our classes here, at his school campus, he lent us a few rooms and this office,' he gestured at the gloomy room they were presently occupying.

'That explains part of the mystery,' Dita said. 'My appointment letter shows the address of this school as the address of Phulpukur College.' She gave an unamused chuckle. 'That is why, while I was asking for directions to the college, people were giving me such strange looks.... There is no college to speak of!'

'There is a college,' Palash sounded brusque, almost rude, 'classes are already on, our first batch will appear for board examinations this year. You just need to settle yourself in!'

Dita was baffled, 'But you just said I'm the first teacher appointed to this college. So who has been teaching the students?'

'We have an army of part-time teachers,' the latest entrant into the room, a cheerful man dressed in formal black trousers and a crisp white shirt, replied. His body language exuded easy confidence as he deftly drew out another chair and joined the group at the table. 'Let me introduce myself,' he smiled. 'I'm Devdutt Sarkar, headmaster, Saint James. Phulpukur College has been nurtured on my campus for almost two years now. I know it will be a struggle, but we are all there to support you, don't worry.

'Plans for the college building are well in place, funds have been released too,' continued Devdutt, blissfully unaware of Palash's baleful glance. 'I would suggest that the governing body of the college sanction three signatories to allocate and disburse funds whenever required, so that it does not become a headache for Miss Roy.'

Dita nodded absent-mindedly, somewhat reassured that she would not be burned at the stake over financial matters, which were not her area of expertise. She tried to move the discussion to familiar ground. 'Do I get to meet my class today? And can I please have the college timetable?'

While the others sat huddled in stony-faced gloom, Salim dug out a folder from a heap of dusty folders strewn on the table, opened it up to a yellowing page and handed it to her. Holding the folder cautiously, Dita tried to make sense of the handwritten timetable.

'I'll ask our head clerk to type it out for you, the master copy is on the school noticeboard....' Salim added helpfully.

Typed or handwritten, Dita could not believe her eyes. 'But there is no class allocated to English in this timetable,' she exclaimed. By now, matters were spinning out of control, well beyond her ambit of understanding.

'There is a Compulsory English class,' Palash pointed out, a note of condescension evident in his tone, as if he were doing her a favour by allocating this class to her.

'You mean to tell me you need a full-time lecturer for a Compulsory English class...one class, once a week?' Dita's voice rose steadily, her disbelief mounting with every ascending note. She felt as if she was drowning in the murky waters of Phulpukur, with not even a straw to clutch at. 'This college does not offer English honours or even English as a subject choice in the pass course graduation degree?'

'Who will study English here? It is not even taught properly at the school level...and all of us come from local Bengali-medium schools! We can just about sign our names in English,' Pinku pointed out. 'Never really had a proper English teacher in our schools.'

'Why did the college apply for a post in English, then?' Dita fumed.

Both Palash and Devdutt appeared sheepish, and because Dita was so obviously waiting for an answer, and as no one really wanted to spell it out, Mukul opened his mouth for the first time in this awkward encounter. 'They wanted someone with good English language skills to take care of the correspondence that goes on almost on a daily basis between the college and the Ministry of Education and

College Service Commission to secure funds for the college, obtain university grants, introduce new subjects.... Most of the time our petitions are simply rejected because no one can understand the gibberish that we write. There is no one to edit or proofread our petitions and, obviously, no one to write them in the first place.'

'Hmmm.... What you need is a glorified clerk. You could just have applied for one?' Dita observed curtly, trying to infuse some sense into the madness, which seemed to be rapidly engulfing her.

With a frown, Mukul replied, 'We already have the entire office staff, appointed by the government. Two clerks, one accountant, a librarian, and an office boy...and let me assure you that even if they pooled all their intellectual resources together, they wouldn't be able to come up with a single grammatically correct English sentence.'

He looked straight into her eyes, 'Now you can understand our plight, perhaps? We need to send comprehensive petitions to the Ministry of Education to ensure the development of this college. Till now our applications must have been pretty incomprehensive, I suppose, as we haven't received any replies.... We need you to step up and work for the benefit of Phulpukur College.'

Heads were bobbing up and down around the table in agreement with Mukul's ardent appeal. Dita, however, was far from convinced. 'Why didn't you ensure that your clerks are fluent in English when you knew that they would have to be in charge of all correspondence on behalf of the college? If your accountant does not have a sound knowledge of English you can manage, but surely it is imperative that the clerks have a working knowledge of the language?'

A long silence followed Dita's query. No one seemed to be in a rush to answer her. Palash was about to speak when something suddenly caught his attention; his face froze into a grim mask of disapproval.

Dita looked around to see that the friendly young man had finally resurfaced with a tea tray, followed by Gopal carrying an assortment of snacks. This accounted for the delay, Dita thought, he must have gone to procure the refreshments. As the aroma of the freshly brewed tea wafted across the room, she realized that she was rather hungry.

ৎ

It had been a long drive from Kolkata to Phulpukur. Dita had started off before daybreak, armed with a road map provided by her mother, Tamali, who had very little faith that Dita's GPS would be able to find its way in rural Bengal. She had wanted to accompany Dita on her first day at her new job, but Dita managed to fob her off—on top of everything else, she did not want her mother on her back. It had been a long haul to reach this point, she thought, as she threw in her holdall and eased into the driver's seat of her Maruti. She had put in a lot of effort to qualify for, then pass the National Eligibility Test, and then get through the mind-boggling rounds of interviews with the College Service Commission.

Driving out of Salt Lake, she circumnavigated half of Kolkata using the Eastern Metropolitan Bypass, after which it was all Martian landscape to her as strange locations whizzed past, places that she had never visited nor heard of. Not a single driver seemed to abide by traffic rules known to civilized men; they drove with reckless abandon without a care for the safety of fellow drivers or pedestrians as if they were being chased by hounds from hell. As she headed into Phulpukur, the warning light on her dashboard was flashing a frenzied red—she was low on petrol.

⌒

Dragging her attention back to the present situation, she observed Palash turn apoplectic with rage as he watched the Tea Boy and Gopal place the trays on the table. Completely ignoring the fact that Palash seemed on the verge of throttling him, the Tea Boy poured out cups of a favourite Bengali beverage—a strong brew of Darjeeling tea with a dash of milk, enhanced with a hint of sugar, which many Bongs enjoy at any time of day.

Amidst all the gloom and doom of the day, this tea break seemed to be the only bright spot for Dita. Her eyes met the warm grey ones of the Tea Boy, her appreciation evident in her smile as she buried her face into the fragrant cup. Smiling with pleasure at her silent gratitude, Raja paused for a moment and pointed at the tableau frozen around the table. 'They will not be able to answer your question,' he chuckled. 'It's a fiasco of their own making.... They have appointed their family members to fill up all the posts in the college office. Nepotism absolved any requirement to know English.'

His mocking laughter echoed down the corridors as he left the miserable bunch to come to terms with this chaos of their own creation. While the others looked sheepish, Palash looked positively furious. If looks could kill, Tea Boy would have been well on his way to the gates of hell. Although he didn't seem at all bothered at incurring Palash's wrath, Papu's heart went out to the young man: Palash's enmity would be a terrible cross to bear.

Dita did not know which way to look, although by now she should have been immune to the shocks of the day. She wondered what trick the kurta-dhoti gang would next pull out of their sleeves in this never-ending farce.

'It's not nepotism,' Palash fumed. 'You have to understand that we need to provide proper employment to the boys of our village. And if they were qualified enough for the posts, should we have deprived them only because they happen to be related to us?'

Devdutt shared the same view. 'To secure a government job is far from easy these days. We were merely empowering our village youth with these placements.'

'And who exactly did you choose to empower in your benevolence?' Dita could not hold back the sarcasm any longer.

'The head clerk, Alok Pundit, is our cousin,' Papu and Pinku's voices rose in unison. 'This college is our grandfather's dream project, and Alok represents our family in this mission. He is a graduate, so you cannot contest the fact that he deserves the post.'

'Praloy Nath is the second clerk, he is Mukul dada's son,' continued Pinku. 'Our accountant Ashok Mondol is Salim's friend, the librarian Dipten Ghosh is Devdutt dada's brother-in-law, and the office boy, Biltu, is my wife's brother.'

They have it nicely sorted, Dita thought, almost as if they were running a family business. Unable to contain her curiosity any further, she asked Pinku, 'And what exactly do you do? Besides being a member of the governing body here?'

Rather pleased at having secured her undivided attention, Pinku eagerly provided his job profile. 'Papu and I work for Shyamol Sathi. You will find us at the party office all through the week.'

'Yes, yes, we all know just how efficient you two are,' Palash sounded extremely irritated as he rose to leave, bringing the meeting to an abrupt end.

Palash did not seem to have any progeny or distant relative employed in the college, Dita noticed. Or had she overlooked any link?

'Is Biltu, the office boy, the one who brought in tea this morning?' she wondered out loud, captivated by the Tea Boy's intriguing and irreverent presence.

Palash stiffened, a red haze of impotent fury clouding his vision. Dita's guileless query made him choke on the answer—he decided to remain silent.

'No, that's not Biltu,' Devdutt replied uneasily. 'He's a former student of mine and sometimes comes over to meet me. We play chess when I am free, it's an interesting diversion from the regular administrative work.' He had a fond look in his eyes but did not mention the Tea Boy's name.

As the dhoti-gang started to troop out of the room, Palash looked back and paused for a moment. 'You are an essential part of Phulpukur now, Miss Roy...wearing a sari might help you assimilate better to the ways of this world.'

Palash's sucker punch left Dita reeling. What had she really signed up for? Picking up her keys, she walked quickly to her car.

Somewhere on the distant fringes of her conscious mind she saw Tea Boy caught in a heated argument with Palash Bose.

She got into her car and drove off. She couldn't get away from this crazy place fast enough.

2

The Over Story

Stepping out of the school gate, Papu and Pinku made their way to the heart of the village, the local haat, where farmers and their wives gathered to sell vegetables, fruits, and fish on certain days of the week. Meat was a delicacy, and only two stalls at the rear end of the haat sold chicken and mutton, but not on Thursdays due to local rules.

The smell of decaying greens or the malodorous whiffs of air circulating the stench of fish left out in the sun for too long were not a deterrent, however, to people devoting their lives to politics. Thus, the Phulpukur haat was flanked on one side by a brand new, rather ostentatious building—the party office of Shyamol Sathi. This conspicuous structure painted in emerald green and an array of whites was the diurnal habitat of the Pundit twins.

The twins were gregarious souls, comfortable in their own skins, yet with an uncanny resemblance to their bloodthirsty ancestor in the sardonic bent of arched black eyebrows or the way in which, unconsciously, they looked down their hawkish noses. Loose limbed and tall, they moved with identical leopard-like grace; theirs was an earthy, instinctive existence unfiltered by excessive intellectual aspirations, their almond-shaped eyes reflecting startling clarity and a strange mix of world-weariness.

'You did not mention Sahana's name even once,' Papu said softly, eyeing Pinku quizzically.

'What's there to mention?' Pinku's voice showed his lack of interest.

Papu, obviously in a breezier mood than Pinku, snickered, 'You got all intimidated by the mention of nepotism. You mentioned Biltu, but you failed to disclose the fact that your wife is one of the part-time teachers in the college.'

Papu seemed to enjoy Pinku's discomfort; he knew Sahana's choice of profession was a bone of contention in his twin's marital relationship. Being the only daughter of the village postmaster, Sahana had literally fought every inch of the way to secure her education. Her father supported her as much as he could until she graduated from a college in Kolkata, after which he refused to budge from his desire to see her married off to some nice chap. This nice chap turned out to be Pinku, who had been running around in circles, following Sahana like a lovesick puppy, while she, blissfully unaware of his existence, travelled back and forth from Kolkata.

Eventually, Pinku's father found out that his son was spending a good part of his days moping around the village bus stop, waiting for Sahana to board or alight from the Kolkata bus. And since, by the look of things, his son was not making much headway, Aditya Pundit decided to take matters into his own hands and approached Sahana's father.

Sahana's father, Satish Ghosh, could not have expected a better match. The Pundits were one of the wealthiest families of the village, and Pinku was a scion of that illustrious family. In Satish's scheme of things, this would be a match made in heaven. Besides this, Aditya Pundit magnanimously declared that he was only concerned with his son's happiness and was not seeking even a dime as dowry.

Sahana's fate was sealed. In vain did she try to convince her father that she wanted to study further. When all her protests fell on deaf ears, she tried another line of argument: 'All that this chap does is spend time in the Shyamol Sathi party office, he has never even gone to college...he actually does nothing.' Satish remained stubborn, 'He doesn't need to do much.... The kind of family that he comes from, no one will be surprised if he becomes an important political figure one of these days.'

Pinaki Pundit aka Pinku was married off to his dream girl with much pomp and gaiety, and Sahana was reconciled to live out her life according to the demands of parental expectations. Fortunately, the marriage did not turn out to be as miserable as she had expected. She was quickly drawn into the easy camaraderie that flowed between the twins. Faces crowned by unruly mops of bouncy hair, they were hopelessly identical; even their thought processes traversed along similar lines. Their world view was quite simple: follow whatever comes easily, and be satisfied with what you have. Good for them, Sahana thought. They never had to struggle to achieve anything, everything comes easily to them—except university degrees!

Sahana never did figure out how to be a perfect wife; she had very little interest in the traditional roles of a cook, cleaner, and lover all rolled into one. Pinku did not seem to have great expectations in this regard, he was in awe of his erudite wife, and head over heels in love with her. He considered it a privilege to find her at home after he came back from endless hours of political deliberations in the

Shyamol Sathi party office. Following his brother's lead, Papu tried his best to like this arrogant girl and found comfort in his brother's happiness. However, a serpent was soon to enter this blissful Garden of Eden...and it arrived in the form of job vacancies in Phulpukur College.

One fine morning Pinku found his wife eagerly poring over *The Statesman*, the Kolkata-based English newspaper that had an entire page dedicated to job vacancies in West Bengal; she was busy underlining segments of that page with a pencil. As he approached her, curious to know what she was up to, her face lit up with excitement and he was quickly enveloped in an impulsive hug. Apparently, an advertisement had appeared for vacancies for teaching jobs in Phulpukur College—the college required a host of part-time teachers. This was one of the best opportunities for her, Sahana explained, she would be putting in her application.

Enjoying the comfort of that blissful embrace, Pinku did not want to disillusion her. He did not tell her that he knew about the posts that were coming up in the college; after all, he was a member of the governing body, complicit in all organizational decisions. But he had kept this detail to himself; he did not want to raise false hopes in his wife's mind. Pinku knew his father would never agree to the idea of a female member of the Pundit family seeking employment; he would consider it a disgrace to his family.

Aditya Pundit's face assumed the darkness of an imminent thunderstorm when he was apprised of Sahana's intentions. Round upon round of emergency family meetings ensued, where the rest of the family sought to make Sahana understand the traditional role of women in the Pundit household. Unfortunately, the more they ganged up on her, the less obliging she became, and in the spirit of a true-blue rebel, she mailed her CV to the college office. The Pundit patriarchs realized that they had bitten off more than they could chew. Sahana's intransigence gained her a secret admirer: Papu was amazed at the way the intrepid girl fought back to assert her rights; she also secured her mother-in-law Radha's grudging admiration.

'Let her go, let her do something that she can do,' Radha persuaded Aditya, 'considering the fact that she can neither cook nor clean and has no interest whatsoever in household matters, she might as well go and teach in this college.... Anyway, she seems to be the only family member who wants to participate in the educational aspect of the college,' she scoffed, 'the rest of you are only interested in politics or the business that it will bring.'

Aditya sat speechless as Radha ended her petition on a sentimental note, 'I tell you, she is going to be the true representative of this family in Phulpukur College, we can all live the dream with her.... And Durjoy Pundit will be a happy soul in heaven.' Here she paused, for impact, and raised her eyes heavenwards, as if to seek blessings from the departed soul.

Eventually, Sahana was called for an interview, secured the post of part-time lecturer in Political Science, and the rest, as they say, is history. Along with Sahana, seven other candidates were appointed to teach various subjects, but she was the only woman in the team. Until Dita showed up, that is.

Papu completely empathized with his brother's confusion. Pinku did not know whether to be proud of his wife or cower under the burden of his father's obvious disapproval.

Mostly he left things unsaid, but somewhere deep in his heart he understood that his wife had been able to secure respect even in the eyes of the egotistic Palash Bose, who was almost always openly disdainful of Pinku's intellect, or lack thereof.

Sahana, in her wisdom, had tried to remedy this situation, and enrolled the twins for a correspondence course in advanced English. And so it was that Papu and Pinku were facing a gauntlet of linguistic challenges, sitting in the Shyamol Sathi Party office every evening and racking their brains over seemingly unsolvable grammatical dilemmas. Sometimes, they caught hold of unsuspecting party members who stepped into the office for a game or two of carrom, but rarely did they get adequate help, the English language and its complexities being a puzzle to all and sundry.

However, there were some good days. Few and far between, but still, better than most. Days on which the people who came to the party office actually knew adequate English. No wonder, then, when Anupam Bose breezed in, the twins could hardly conceal their delight. He was the gift horse who could make them pass the nerve-wracking test they were supposed to take today to advance to the next level in the correspondence course.

Anupam Bose was Palash Bose's older son, known to everyone in Phulpukur as Pom. His disconcertingly clear grey eyes lit up with curiosity over an impish smile as he saw the twins frowning over their computer screens. Unlike his father, he was vivacious and friendly, ever ready to crack a joke or fire off an amusing retort.

'Pom,' boomed Pinku, 'you are a fucking godsend, bro,' while Papu dragged him to sit next to the computers where they were about to sign in for the test.

Pinku's eyebrows shot up. 'Bro!' he chuckled, 'Papu is being educated at last.... By an unhealthy diet of English movies.'

'Is God sanctioning cheating nowadays?' Pom asked good-humouredly, well aware of the twins' plight. 'Sahana should have enrolled you in the elementary course. Not all the films in this world will be able to drill English into your heads,' he continued, only to be rudely nudged by a pair of elbows while two faces looked at him expectantly, with absolute faith that he would make them pass the test.

Pom sighed dramatically; he had no alternative but to solve their problems. Once the test was done, and they had been cleared to ascend to the next level of difficulty, the twins decided it was time to pay some actual attention to Pom.

'How come you're here today, Pom, in the middle of the week?' asked Papu. Everyone in Phulpukur knew that Pom worked for a software firm in Kolkata and came back to his village once or twice a month during the weekends. His presence in Phulpukur on a weekday indeed deserved a query.

'Daddy Bose is driving me bonkers,' Pom groaned. 'He wants me to get married.... Apparently, he has managed to find a girl of his choice, with appropriate family pedigree and he wants me to go and see her. Tomorrow!'

'Why this sudden desperation to get you married right now?' wondered Pinku. 'Surely it can wait until you find someone you really like?'

'Palash Bose never ceases to amaze,' sniggered Papu, 'why is he so worried about pedigree? Considering the fact that he himself did not even marry into a Bengali family, he shouldn't be talking about pedigree…. Besides, it sounds as if he is trying to marry you off to a dog or something.'

'Stop dragging my mother's family into my father's mess,' Pom said angrily. 'My father has always been a problem for Ma, with his never-ending expectations, but she never complains.'

Papu and Pinku were aware that Palash Bose's family had fallen into an acute financial crisis. Palash's father, Bikram Bose, had moved to Phulpukur when Palash was very young. Bikram became quite well known to the villagers as one of the best maths teachers in Saint James School. Fitting into the archetypal image of the eccentric mathematician, Bikram's life was dedicated to the love of numbers; he hardly had any time or inclination to worry about the economic condition of his family. By the time his two daughters were of marriageable age, Bikram had scarcely any money saved to arrange for respectable weddings. To extricate himself out of a gradually worsening situation, Bikram managed to secure a match for his son with a girl from an affluent Marwari business family in Kolkata, in exchange for a handsome dowry and the promise of a secure share in their business. The Marwaris of Rajasthan dominate much of the business set-ups in Kolkata, and the Pugalia family agreed to marry off a daughter of their family for one reason.

Hemlata dragged her left foot when she walked, her left leg being a couple of inches shorter than her right. This disability became a major challenge, reducing her value in the marriage market. Thus, when Palash's father proposed the match, the Pugalias heaved a sigh of relief. It was a marriage of convenience. A fact that Palash kept reminding his two sons about whenever he thought that they were not mindful enough of the sacrifice he had made for his family.

Wallowing in self-pity at being saddled with a lame wife, Palash seldom acknowledged the fact that if one looked beyond the obvious physical disadvantage, one would realize that Hemlata possessed a shrewd business sense which aided many of Palash's speculations and investments. Besides, she was a strikingly beautiful woman with a comely figure and a pretty face, framed by a tumble of dark curly hair, which she often tied back with strings of jasmine or wild roses. But her languid grey eyes were her most striking feature, which, when lit up with a smile, could penetrate right into your soul. She came like a breath of fresh air to the waning fortunes of the Bose family. Hemlata would definitely have earned a much better match than Palash, if only she could stand properly on her own two feet, as she herself admitted wryly.

The only good outcome of this obviously lopsided marriage were her sons, who were genetically blessed with her good looks, a keen sense of humour, and reasonable intellect. Unfortunately, the more the boys resembled Hemlata, the more they tended to fall foul of Palash.

Now it was Pom's turn to be in the line of fire. Palash had turned a deaf ear to his protestations, and Pom had been unceremoniously summoned from Kolkata to meet the girl of his father's choice and quite possibly finalize his marriage.

'Caught between the devil and the deep blue sea,' Pom sighed ruefully.

'Who is this girl?' the twins were all agog. 'Go see her, and if you don't like her, just say so.'

But Pom was uneasy. 'I don't like this idea of arbitrarily walking into someone's house to see some random stranger.... It's creeping me out! And no, I have no clue who the girl is.'

Papu felt sorry for Pom. 'I can come with you, if you want?' he offered hesitantly.

'Try to steer clear from Palash kaka today, Pom,' advised Pinku. 'He wasn't happy with the way things were shaping up in the meeting with Dita Roy today at Phulpukur College. He's on a short fuse.'

Feeling rather relieved that Papu would be there to help him out tomorrow, Pom got up to leave. 'My father is hardly ever in a good mood nowadays,' he sighed. 'And who is this Dita Roy who is adding fuel to the fire?'

'She has been appointed as a full-time lecturer in English in Phulpukur College.... Poor girl, she seemed to be at her wits' end when she found out that the college does not even have an English department to speak of!' Papu could not hold back a smile at the sheer irony of the situation.

Pom stood at the door, nonplussed. 'Why did you guys sanction a post for English? The governing body knows that there is no English department, right?' Unconsciously, he was echoing the same concern that Dita had raised during the meeting a few hours earlier.

Papu and Pinku refrained from pointing out the obvious answer: the decisions of the governing body were mostly unilateral, and this one, like so many of them, was Palash Bose's brainchild.

Pom was intelligent enough to interpret the silence. Shrugging ruefully as he left the room, he added, 'I think I saw her.... While I was driving past Saint James, I saw a woman in blue almost running towards her car as if she was being pursued by the hounds of hell. Now I know why.

'And she was easy on the eye.... Like a willow in the wind.'

3

Home and the World

'If you ever write an autobiography, the title for this chapter in your life would be something like "My Experiments with Life" or "Skirmishes Bordering on Insanity",' Tamali could hardly control her laughter, her fine-boned, heart-shaped face turning red with the effort. 'Imagine trying to teach English in a college where no one understands the language, and there is no actual department dedicated to English!'

In her mid-fifties, but surprisingly youthful in her appearance, Tamali was a vivacious woman, with a keen awareness about everything in life; her children would often joke about the prominent red bindi that adorned her alabaster forehead—it was her third eye, they would say, eternally awake and observant. Tamali would laugh along with them, but bringing up her children almost single-handedly, she could not afford to be unaware of anything happening in their lives. She treasured the companionship of her children and though they were not a particularly demonstrative family, they valued their warm and supportive relationship.

Tamali's wicked sense of humour could sometimes be the bane of Dita's existence, at other times it could end up salvaging an otherwise bleak and unsettling day. More specifically, a day such as this.

'You are partly to blame, you must acknowledge that,' Tamali reflected. 'Were you really expecting to find a full-fledged English department in a college located in the middle of nowhere?'

Carving a wholesome piece of roasted chicken, mildly seasoned with basil and thyme, Tamali served her daughter and her son, Dita and Arko, as the three of them settled down for dinner. Munching on a warm and buttery piece of garlic bread, Dita managed to insulate herself from the madness of the day. 'You should have seen the look on Palash Bose's face, Mom. He must have been expecting someone mediocre and pliable enough to resolve their clerical issues. He thought that only a man would take on this job; apparently, not many women are interested in securing posts that take them out of Kolkata. He certainly wasn't expecting someone like me.'

Tamali smiled; she could guess the kind of havoc her free-spirited child had unleashed on the unsuspecting villagers. 'I don't want to say I told you so, but you really needed to think twice or maybe thrice before you accepted the post, Dita. Instead, you charged into this village like Don Quixote tilting at windmills.'

Arko couldn't hold back a fit of giggles; picturing his sister as a crazed knight in shining armour was too much for him to handle.

'Poor, unsuspecting Palash Bose...he won't know what hit him by the time you are done with him.' Tamali's delicate lips curved into an indulgent smile, the multiple silver bangles on her wrists clinked as she rested her cheeks on her hands and astutely observed, 'You won't be fobbed off with measly classes or admin work, even a blind man can see that!'

Dita shrugged her shoulders ruefully, aware that she did not have much of a choice. Over the last two years, hardly any vacancies had opened up for permanent placements in the colleges of Kolkata, forcing her to look further afield for a job.

In fact, Phulpukur seemed to be a lesser evil—it was an hour-and-a-half drive from Kolkata—in comparison to the other posts available for general candidates. Most of the vacancies were located in the deltas of Sundarbans or remote places in North Bengal. Candidates taking up posts in such places would have to relocate there and embark on a new life, almost on a new planet. At least from Phulpukur, Dita would be able to return home every evening.

Coming back home every day was an absolute must for Dita. Her father's job kept him mostly out of Kolkata, and Tamali herself had a hectic work schedule, so someone had to ensure that Arko was not left alone at home. He was still too young to fend for himself.

Tamali's phone vibrated—all phones in the Roy household were perpetually in silent mode. The Roys had to see the call on their screens and then, if they wanted to take the call, they would pick up the phone. And there was an unspoken rule of not accepting calls at dinner time. It was the only meal of the day when the entire family sat down together. However, today was an exception to the rule, because the person calling was Dita's father. Tamali answered the call.

'Arnab, high time you called…. Dita is hyperventilating… that job of hers has landed her in a strange situation. Apparently, she has to take charge as the acting principal and handle the administrative affairs of the college. To make matters worse, the college does not even have an English department, so basically, she has nothing to teach!' Tamali smiled into the phone as Arnab replied to her outburst. 'Yes, yes, I know you are her spiritual guru and all! Try and make her see the light?' she laughed and handed the phone to Dita.

Dita's cup of sorrow truly overflowed now, and her father lent her a patient ear. Finally, after ten long minutes of offering his silent and unconditional support, Arnab broke in, 'You need to get a grip on the situation, darling. I know you have always been enthusiastic about teaching, but you should also be aware that initial placements in government jobs are not always very cushy ones.... If you think that my position at the beginning of my career was peachy, forget it!'

Arnab was an archaeologist and had fought tooth and nail to claw his way up to the highest echelons of the Archaeological Survey of India. His job had taken him to the strangest of places in the subcontinent as well as across the world, places where he could not possibly expect his family to accompany him. It was Tamali who had single-handedly brought up the children. As a result, she could not pursue her career in group theatre, despite having been a promising actress in her youth. Recently, however, she had ventured into essaying small roles in a spate of web series, which were becoming rather popular nowadays. Adding to the small pleasures of life was the fact that Arko was thrilled to bits—his mother was a celebrity in his eyes.

While Arnab was still busy soothing a disillusioned and crestfallen daughter, Tamali served a round of lemon mousse; she loved to cook, and her children dug in unabashedly.

Poor Arnab could only see the delicious dishes on screen and signed off with a dramatic sigh.

The three of them took their time to polish off the dessert while Arko kept them entertained with hilarious episodes from his school. He was just fifteen, but at times wise beyond his age. Somewhat on the chubby side, he was just coming to terms with the fact that girls in his class preferred the tall, dark, handsome kind of guys. 'And I don't fit into any of these categories,' he whispered in mock horror. 'I'm short and have no idea whether I'll grow a few inches to make myself somewhat presentable! I am not very dark at all, and I would rather not comment on the handsome part!'

He paused for a moment, dramatically. 'And then I thought, who cares? Let me make myself pleasing to me first! I am not even sure I want to put any effort into chasing those silly girls.' Some of the gloom that had engulfed Dita was borne away by a spate of laughter.

'Any pleasing moments from your day, Dita?' Tamali asked kindly, 'or was it just downhill all the way?'

'Storm in a teacup,' Arko quipped. 'Didi knows how to hold the fort.'

'Teacups and a pair of deep grey eyes,' Dita smiled, her face lighting up with the memory. 'The only good things from today.'

'Grey eyes, hmmm?' Tamali considered the point gravely. 'And on whom did you find such grey eyes in the back of beyond, if we may ask?'

Ignoring her mother's question Dita replied, 'I still don't know his name; he brought me a cup of tea this morning and then got my car refuelled too! I haven't even paid him for the petrol,' Dita added guiltily. She made a mental note to ask Palash Bose how to make the payments to the Tea Boy, since he did not appear to be employed either by Phulpukur College or Saint James School.

Palash Bose sometimes felt like an alien in his own house, especially on days when both his sons were intent on ganging up on him at the dinner table. The moment Hemlata called out 'Anupam, Anuraj, dinner is ready' and he heard the boys talking excitedly as they came down from their rooms, he knew he was in for trouble. He tried to solve this problem to the best of his ability by putting his chin up and assuming the demeanour of a medieval potentate.

Hemlata was perhaps the only person in the entire village who insisted on calling her sons by their given names, no one else bothered, and their names had been conveniently abridged to Pom and Raja. Undaunted by the cold vibes Palash imagined himself as giving off, Pom and Raja dragged chairs noisily and settled on either side of their recalcitrant father. As three pairs of quizzical, deep-grey eyes zeroed in on him, Palash's frown deepened. It was abundantly clear that he would be subjected to a deluge of unnecessary queries.

'You have made a habit of making fools out of unsuspecting people,' the youngest pair of grey eyes led the assault, ignoring the piping hot dal, roti, and rajma that had been laid out on the table. His shoulders went stiff with disapproval: food could wait, there were many other problems to be dealt with first.

'Hemlata,' Palash roared, 'you really need to control Raja, he rushes in, uninvited, to all sorts of awkward situations and ends up making things abjectly difficult for me.'

Hemlata did not seem unduly disturbed by Palash's accusation. 'What have you done now, Anuraj?' she asked softly.

'The wretched boy was already there when we went to meet Dita Roy,' Palash fumed. 'Let quite a few cats out of the bag today, I'm sure, and almost sabotaged the meeting, feeding information to that clueless woman, where none was required. The last thing I can expect from my family is discretion.'

Hemlata turned pale, cringing from the bitterness implicit in her husband's words. Palash had never been able to control Raja. Unlike Pom, who at least tried to pretend that he was obeying his father, Raja was a bag of mischief, charging at Palash with heretical glee wherever and whenever he thought his father was doing something wrong. And since Palash habitually ended up doing all the wrong things, the battle of wills and wits between these two continued unabated. Hemlata already knew that they had had a mighty falling out that morning too.

'But why were you there, Anuraj?' Hemlata persisted.

'I was curious,' Raja replied, a contemplative look washing away the belligerence from the clear grey of his eyes. 'I wanted to see who this person was who was coming down all the way from Kolkata to join Phulpukur College. It's usually the other way around, isn't it...? People from this village are desperate to leave and go to cities.'

Raja paused, reliving that moment of consternation when he saw a rather tired young woman step out of her Maruti; he had looked on with wonder as she pulled her diminutive form together with surprising resolution and started walking towards the school campus. Lamb to the slaughter, he thought, and he simply couldn't resist the idea of seeing her up close.

Palash broke into his reverie. 'The boy is incorrigible; he went in to meet Dita Roy on the pretext of serving her tea.'

Pom could hardly hold back his laughter—only Raja could pull such tricks. 'Methinks, I saw the lady too...very easy on the eyes I must say.'

Raja winked at him across the table.

Palash smirked, 'No need to be so happy, she thought you were some random tea-bearer or something.'

Pom burst out laughing, 'And I am sure you did not correct the situation, Baba, did you?'

'Why should I?' Palash demurred, glowing at his pyrrhic victory. 'He shouldn't have been there in the first place, propagating ideas of nepotism.'

Raja looked sheepish as Pom chortled, 'Raja the tea-bearer.... What brew did you serve, Raja? Judging by her looks, that lady will only have Earl Grey or English Breakfast!'

Raja blanched, 'Not even Darjeeling First Flush, I just picked up a box of tea leaves from the school canteen; but I think she enjoyed it as a welcome diversion from the catastrophe that was unfolding around her.'

'Better remain the anonymous tea boy then,' suggested Pom playfully. 'Since you haven't been able to make much of a mark in your first appearance.'

'Dinner is getting cold, boys,' Hemlata chided as she urged her sons to fill their plates. As the boys dug into their food, Palash helped himself half-heartedly; even after so many years of marriage he had not been able to summon up enthusiasm for what he considered to be essentially non-Bengali food. Roti and rajma did not feature at all in the Bengali gastronomic universe; however, his eyes lit up when a tureen of rohu fish curry and a tray of steaming hot rice and green-mango chutney were added to the table. He dug in with gusto.

'You're a fine one to talk,' Hemlata teased Pom. 'I don't think you even know the name of the girl that you are supposed to meet tomorrow.'

'What's in a name?' Raja quoted. 'A rose by any other name would smell as sweet. But is he really interested in any other girl?' Raja said slyly. 'He was just telling me that he thought Dita Roy was rather pretty, he was quite amused by her animated behaviour.'

'What you call animated behaviour was actually beating a hasty retreat from the bunch of madcaps she met at the college, led by your father,' Hemlata couldn't resist taking a dig.

Listening to their lazy banter, Palash was rapidly losing his appetite. 'I don't understand how you can find her pretty. She was dripping arrogance all over the place.'

Pom and Raja understood exactly what had happened: Palash Bose disliked argumentative women, and when someone like Dita Roy challenged his authority, he could hardly take it lying down.

'Forget Dita Roy, she is no concern of yours,' Palash said brusquely. 'I have fixed up an appointment with Girish tomorrow; I want Pom to meet his daughter, Mishti. From what I've heard, she is quite good-looking too.'

Raja leaned in towards Pom, 'Misty with a touch of

money, Pom bhaiya! Of course, she has to be attractive. Her father owns several resorts in Diamond Harbour and runs a flourishing fishing company.'

'Fishy people,' Pom muttered. 'Very fishy,' mumbled Hemlata.

Palash continued to eat, all the while bristling with indignation. He wondered what would happen to them if he withdrew his financial support; Pom had just started off on his career and still needed help from the family. It's all very well to spout ideals, but when push comes to shove, it is your father whom you are going to need, he thought.

Turning a blind eye to Pom's gloomy face, Palash announced his intention to start off early the next morning to see Mishti. Palash tried to be hopeful about the outcome; perhaps seeing the girl might change Pom's mind. So many things hung in the balance, issues that he could never divulge to his family; he reminded himself to be cautious around Raja, the madcap was a loose cannon, intent on wreaking mayhem wherever he thought Palash was taking undue advantage.

Right now, the madcap was convinced that he did not want to leave his brother to the tender mercies of their ruthless father. 'I want to see this girl too, I will come with you tomorrow, Pom,' he winked. 'If you will allow me?'

Raja seldom asked for permission, he asserted his opinion and waited for others to react. Palash knew there was simply no point in arguing with him, Raja would definitely not take no for an answer.

Trying to ease the tension building up in the air, Hemlata ruffled Raja's hair. 'You are going around seeing way too many girls,' she teased. 'Go with Pom tomorrow but keep your opinions to yourself. More specifically, do not embarrass your father.' Being habitually ignored by Palash, it did not even strike her that her husband had not even invited her to join the group next day; but when Raja asked her whether she wanted to come along too, she averted the difficult situation by begging off—the excuse being that her legs would be sore after the long journey. What she did not own up to, even to herself, was the relieved look that entered Palash's eyes; he would have the field all to himself and even convince Pom to agree to a marriage of convenience.

'He manages to do that spectacularly, all by himself,' Raja responded with an ill-concealed grimace. 'I might have exacerbated the matter at times, but I am certainly not the instigator.

'Half of the time he is busy ignoring me.... He did not even deem it fit to introduce me to Dita Roy this morning; I suppose his ego took a colossal tumble because she jumped to the conclusion that I was the tea boy!'

Palash's face turned red with rage. How on earth can one control this boy? Raja, despite being the youngest member of the family was the most vocal and a complete antithesis of his brother: if Pom was the voice of reason in this family, Raja was the voice of dissent. And no matter how much Palash sought to assert his authority, Raja was always ready to undermine and subvert his plans, bringing him down like a house of cards. And that is exactly what he had done that morning.

While Raja was busy pitting his wits against his father, Pom got up from the table. 'I really must call it a day, I'm absolutely beat.'

He left the three of them to resolve their unresolvable

differences and walked away.

For some reason Palash and Raja appear to be perpetually at each other's throats nowadays, Pom brooded. Maybe it was because Raja was straining at the leash to free himself from his father's dominance, while Palash was equally obdurate in his desire to rein him in. This father–son relationship was fraught with difficulties, to the point that Raja, while still a child, had run away from home a couple of times, causing endless worry to the family; finally, Hemlata had convinced Palash to let Raja stay with his uncles in Kolkata and admitted him to La Martiniere School for boys.

La Martiniere was an upscale city school and Palash was far from happy about the drain on his pocket; matters worsened when Pom, who was always very close to Raja, began to miss his brother way too much. Hemlata had to step in again and send her older son to Kolkata too.

With Palash managing to wash his hands of both his sons, Hemlata's brothers took charge and the two boys grew up in the Pugalia household while Palash and Hemlata stayed on in Phulpukur.

Pom, who had all the scholarly tendencies of his father, was an exceptional student, effortlessly sailing through his school years. Raja, however, was the proverbial problem child. Lessons delivered in a class full of unimaginative people failed to ignite even a rudimentary spark of interest. Year after year, he just managed to hang on, overshadowed by his brilliant brother, yet totally comfortable in his skin.

The only time he came alive was when he was playing chess; and then he was all aflame and his existence took an edgy and challenging turn. It was Hemlata who had introduced him to the game, and Raja took to it like a fish to water. His was a razor-sharp mind when it came to matters of chess; soon he was playing at state level and his successes were reported in *Modern Chess Magazine* and *ChessBase India*.

Years of coping with mediocrity had made Raja somewhat of a recluse, an introvert who habitually shied away from the intrusive curiosity of the press and news media. Thus, while his name began to appear in articles, he himself was never available for interviews and his personal life was jealously guarded and kept under wraps.

Throughout his school years, Raja pored over his chessboard and as a result his academics went for a toss. Luckily for him, he secured admission in a reputed college in Kolkata because of his proficiency in chess and went on to play at the national level, participating in the National Premier Chess Championship for two consecutive years. Hemlata accompanied Raja to championship venues in Jammu and Patna, where he finished very near the top.

'No one cares about people who finish very near the top.... Either you are the topper or nothing at all,' Raja told his mother when he took the decision to drop out of formal education after his graduation. He decided it was time for him to dedicate himself totally to this game. He signed on to a couple of online chess academies, told his father that he was taking a year's break, and spent most of his time honing his game. His target was the Aeroflot Open, an open chess tournament held annually in Moscow.

Predictably, Palash was far from happy with Raja's decision. To him it seemed that Raja was on a self-destructive path—it was doubtful whether the boy would achieve anything significant despite his passion for the game. Palash turned to Hemlata for help, 'Ask him to at least take up a job on the side. If he agrees, I can set him up as a part-time teacher in Phulpukur College.'

Raja, as expected, baulked at the very idea. 'Nepotism,' he declared. 'Just because Baba is the president of the governing body does not mean that he can run a family enterprise there.... Besides, I don't have the patience to teach.'

What his parents did not know was that Raja, while enrolling himself for online chess classes, had come up with the idea that it might be worthwhile to open up an online academy of his own, offering interactive chess classes dedicated to teaching openings, strategy, tactics, and endgames to children under fourteen years of age.

Raja soon discovered that Bengali parents firmly believed that a good knowledge of chess would sharpen their children's intellect and develop their powers of concentration. And since Raja was reasonably well known as a national-level chess player, there was a steady flow of subscribers to his classes. And then, Raja chanced upon a brilliant piece of luck: one of his students competed in the World U14 Chess Championship in Montevideo, Uruguay, and secured the position of World Number Three. After this, the floodgates opened; ambitious Bongs were determined to enrol their children with Raja. Everyone wanted to become a champion.

Pom, who had been a silent observer of his brother's exploits until now, gave Raja a sound piece of advice. 'Don't overstretch these classes, it will eat up all the hours that you need for your own training, if you are really aiming for the Aeroflot Open.'

Pom structured Raja's days into well-balanced slots for online tuitions and self-training, leaving time for him to relax, get a breath of fresh air perhaps, or roam around the village if his heart so desired.

Raja's heart, it was now clear to Pom, was up to all kinds of mischief, and he scarcely missed a chance to lock horns with his father. He has made a sport out of it now, he thought ruefully; though he himself did not see eye to eye with his father, Pom never irritated his father intentionally. A fat lot of good it has done me though, he thought, aware that he was to be dragged to see his proposed bride-to-be tomorrow, no matter how unwillingly, to satisfy Palash's idiosyncrasies.

Pom reminded himself to pick up Papu the next morning before they started off for Diamond Harbour. He set the alarm on his phone and settled down to sleep, drifting off to dreams of verdant green fields basking in the last rays of the summer sun as a pretty young girl approached a pristine white car; she stopped before sliding into the driver's seat and glanced up, looking straight at him; her silky brown hair billowed out in the breeze, the robin blue of her kurti clung to her tender form.... His bones seemed to melt with the beauty of the moment...he dived deep into the dream.

4

Point, Counterpoint

*D*ita was working on assimilation today. She had borrowed a sari from her mother and dressed up carefully for the college, but an hour or so into the day, she was convinced that the ground reality of the institution actually dipped below the proverbial zero.

She met Alok and Praloy, two eager young men who manned the college office, which comprised a very small room with four tables and some shelves for storage. The third table was the workspace of the accountant, Ashok, who was busy entering data into an oversized ledger.

'And who occupies the fourth table?' Dita asked. She saw a few books lying on the table and was curious.

'That's mine,' answered Dipten, his face reflecting his perpetually dyspeptic disposition. 'I'm the college librarian.' He looked inexplicably irritated as he picked up the books and arranged them randomly on the table.

A sneaky suspicion stirred in Dita's mind. 'Where is the library? You can perhaps show me?' she asked.

Dipten's face fell like a deflated balloon. 'This is the library,' he mumbled. 'This table and twelve books.'

Dita felt the ground shift beneath her feet, but remained standing, simply because there was no extra chair to collapse onto.

Papu chose this rather unfortunate moment to peep into the office. He had been waiting outside the campus for Pom to pick him up on the way to Diamond Harbour, but Pom was running late so Papu decided to have a cup of tea with the office staff and promptly landed himself in the middle of the fiasco unfolding in the room.

Ashok looked up from the ledger, 'There is no budget to buy books for the library, ma'am; we had applied for a book grant, but that application, as you know, was rejected.' Taking off his glasses, framed with cheap black plastic, and massaging tired bloodshot eyes, he tried to infuse a note of optimism in his voice. 'Now that you are here, I'm sure you will be able to frame applications that will be convincing enough for the University Grants Commission to furnish us with adequate resources.'

In short, she would have to start from scratch to make this college look like an actual college and not a parody of one. Dita blanched as she realized the immensity of the challenges ahead of her.

'Let's step out, some fresh air might help?' Papu suggested, guessing by the look on Dita's face that looked like someone gradually sinking in quicksand.

Once outside, Dita walked briskly towards the gate of the campus, as if she wanted to create as much distance as possible between herself and the college office. 'Will it be a daily dose of horrors like this?' she asked Papu, not really expecting a straight answer. Papu remained silent, waiting for the storm of emotions to subside. 'Am I the only one encountering this huge volley of challenges or is it symptomatic of all the fledgling colleges coming up in West Bengal?'

'Unfortunately, it is,' Papu confirmed. 'The government is pursuing a literacy campaign in dead earnest and is eager to open up colleges in rural Bengal. A few years back it granted permission to many villages to come up with their own colleges, provided that they had an adequate amount of money and land to start off with. The government supplies the rest of the funds and infrastructure, but as you can see, it's a long drawn-out and frustrating process.'

While Dita was mulling over the situation, Papu's attention appeared to have shifted to something else. Turning around she saw a young man waving at Papu. Waving back, with a smile on his face, Papu declared, 'Pom is here, at last!'

Pom walked rapidly towards them, stopping short as he registered the crestfallen look on Dita's face. She was wearing a blue linen sari today; blue must be her favourite colour, he thought. Not really belonging to the namoshkar league, he held out his hand in introduction, 'Hi, I'm Anupam Bose... and you must be Dita!' His face broke into a warm smile, a smile that lit up his eyes and signalled evident appreciation.

Another pair of light eyes, wide-set and deep grey, remarkably similar to those that had charmed her yesterday, she thought, as she shook hands with Pom. But in comparison to the Tea Boy, this man was suave and self-assured, and she saw admiration reflected in his eyes.

Up close she is even prettier, thought Pom as he took in her dainty features, doe-eyed and vulnerable. Right now, however, worry was plastered all over her face. 'What's wrong?' Pom directed his query to Papu, who simply looked at him in uncomfortable silence.

'Nearly everything,' Dita replied in a dull monotone. 'I'm in existential distress!' Beyond this, she did not want to divulge much to a stranger.

'You guys are going somewhere?' Dita had spotted Palash's impatient face peering out of the window of a car parked on the opposite side of the road.

Papu cast a hurried glance at his watch, 'Yes, we are running late, we have to be in Diamond Harbour in half-an-hour.' Casting Dita an apologetic glance at having to leave her in a mess, he beat a hasty retreat towards the car. Palash Bose wasn't someone you kept waiting!

'Guess I'll see you around then,' smiled Pom, before he too loped off towards the waiting car.

Dita was puzzled: she thought she saw the Tea Boy in the driver's seat of the car. She gave herself a mental shake, I'm imagining grey eyes everywhere.

෴

Once he was back in the car, Pom was teased mercilessly by Papu and Raja. Hollering with laughter, Raja said to Papu, 'You should have seen the speed with which Pom jumped out of the car when he saw you talking with Dita Roy.'

'So, how was it brother?' Raja winked at Pom. 'Up close and personal?'

'Shut up, you two,' Pom mumbled. He could literally feel the cold waves of disapproval emanating from Palash who was sitting in the back seat. 'Let's get on our way,' he said; what he actually meant was 'Let's get through this ordeal as quickly as possible.'

Raja turned on the ignition of the car, an ancient Ambassador, which according to him ought to be driven only at vintage car rallies, but like so many other things in his life, Palash refused to buy a more fuel-efficient vehicle.

His line of argument ran thus: 'At this rate you will want to change everything that ages badly. Will you dump your parents too when they get old?' There was simply no logic in arguing this point, and his sons had given up long ago.

By the time the car trundled into the sprawling bungalow by the river Hooghly, they were already an hour late. Eyeing the property Pom felt distinctly uneasy; was his father trying to sell him off to secure this obvious wealth? Girish Sarkar had only one daughter; therefore, she must be the sole heir to his property, which, by the look of things, appeared to be quite substantial.

Girish was waiting under the portico of the house. Dressed in a pristine white dhoti and kurta, offset by an intricately embroidered black Kashmiri shawl on his broad shoulders, his pleasant features lit up with a cherubic smile as he welcomed them and ushered them inside. Raja knew that behind that genial smile, Girish was a shrewd and remarkably astute man who single-handedly managed a flourishing business. What Raja could not begin to fathom was why Girish would feel the need to establish ties between his family and that of Palash Bose, except for the fact that both of them were powerful people in this particular area.

The boys sat huddled together on a plush sofa, somewhat overwhelmed by the opulence of the drawing room they had been invited into. While Girish and Palash were engaged in a conversation regarding Pom's academic qualifications and his future prospects, Raja's mind went into hyper drive trying to figure out the dynamics of the situation.

Meanwhile, Pom and Papu were busy trying to keep up with Palash and Girish's repartee, which was gradually devolving into something like a business deal. They heard

Girish assert rather strongly, 'Listen to me, Palash. I like your son, and I am sure my daughter will like him too, but you have to keep in mind that Mishti might not want to settle for a life in Phulpukur. She has a mind of her own, and I will not be able to convince her otherwise.'

Palash demurred, 'Girish, Pom lives in Kolkata, he has his own apartment out there. In case they like each other well enough to get married, Mishti can live in Kolkata.'

Raja was even more confused; he had hardly ever seen his father bending back so much to give the other person space. Palash must want something more than the money that this marriage deal was sure to bring in.

Two attendants entered the room with trays laden with Mughlai parathas and an assortment of local sweets. The conversation lulled; in the early morning rush to get to Diamond Harbour, the boys had skipped breakfast, and now they happily dug into the hot parathas.

'Thankfully, my father did not say that I have made all of this, to extol my culinary skills,' a cheerful voice sneaked into the room. The three boys looked up to see a pair of amused eyes measuring them up. 'This looks so much like a swayamvar sabha. I must say I wasn't really expecting three young men to pick and choose from,' the girl said as she stopped in front of them. Dressed in a casual salmon-pink salwar kameez, she was imp-thin with hair as black as dark winter nights tumbling down her shoulders in an insane riot of curls. The warm honey of her skin reflected the joie de vivre of a sunny personality; on the whole she did not exactly embody anyone's idea of a blushing bride-to-be.

'Why only pick and choose?' Raja's eyes danced with mischief. 'You can mix and match too!'

The girl spun around to face Raja. 'That's wicked, deliciously wicked,' she said, her initial surprise followed by a tinkle of laughter. 'I like your style, whoever you are, and I choose you,' she pointed at Raja dramatically. 'You will go well with these two in the mix and match section.'

'Father,' she focused on the increasingly contrite looking Girish, 'I have found myself a harem it seems; please sign the deal with the head honcho there,' she indicated Palash. 'And get these boys for me.'

Palash nearly gagged on his food, Raja and Pom rolled with laughter, and Papu looked completely nonplussed.

Desperately seeking to infuse some sanity into a situation that was rapidly getting out of hand, Girish tried to stop his errant daughter. 'Mishti, not all the boys are up for grabs....'

Mishti did not let her father finish, 'Are you saying they will not be cost effective?' She paused, apparently contemplating the complexity of the situation. 'Hmmmmm.... If I can have only one, I think I will settle for him,' again she pointed at Raja.

Palash was struck dumb with consternation; this wasn't going well at all. But before he could react, Papu jumped into the fray. 'You can't have him,' he said with a mournful wail, pulling Raja into a bear hug and refusing to let him go, 'he's mine!'

Palash's jaw dropped to the floor, he could scarcely comprehend what was happening.

While Raja was being smothered in Papu's embrace, Mishti took a quick call, 'It seems this is a "buy one get one free" deal! Suits me fine, I'll take it,' she turned a happy face to her father.

Girish could hardly contain his dismay, 'Even two is

not cost effective,' he used Mishti's lingo to pay her back. 'One is,' he pointed at Pom. 'And only that one.'

I love being objectified, Pom thought with a trace of bitterness as he became the target of Mishti's undivided attention.

'Father chose well,' Mishti declared, eyeing Pom. 'The proverbial tall and handsome guy with light eyes thrown in for good measure.'

Heaving a sigh of relief, Papu let go of Raja.... Thank God, Pom was the chosen one! His relief, however, was short-lived: Palash looked angry enough to throttle him with his bare hands.

'Come, let's go out to the terrace,' Mishti insisted. 'All three of you,' she said, catching their unsure glances. 'You look more like a package deal to me than anything else. Let's leave the oldies to settle their scores...they won't need us around while they sort out the business side of this deal.'

The view from the terrace was breathtaking: the blues of the river Hooghly stretched out to the sheltering skies, a smattering of fishing boats bobbed up and down on the gentle waves, the delicate smell of distant jasmines wafted in the breeze.

Pom was so beguiled by the beauty of the setting that he became even more speechless than usual but Raja could not be impressed so easily. He was chomping at the bit to question Mishti about her less than exemplary behaviour.

'I can sense the queries buzzing around at sonic speed inside your head,' Mishti said to Raja, her smile lighting up her face with a gamine charm.

Raja made up his mind: he definitely liked this quirky girl. 'You're quite a hoot, you know? All those histrionics, you pulled them off quite well too. But jokes apart, tell me, are you really interested in an arranged marriage for yourself?'

Pom turned around and focused his attention on this rather unusual girl, keen to hear her answer. Mishti looked at him with a steady gaze and took her time to answer Raja's question, 'Yes, I am.' She did not seem to be in the mood to expand on that; her attention had now turned to Papu, she looked at him and then at Raja, 'Are you really a couple?' she asked, her eyes glittering with excitement.

'No such luck, Raja won't have me,' Papu replied, eyeing Raja wistfully. Both the brothers ignored him, having eyes only for the girl. Papu moved away in search of some more food.

Now, Pom was insistent, 'Why would you want to opt for an arranged marriage, Mishti? Why not marry a boy of your choice, someone whom you actually know, instead of risking it all with a stranger? We are not living in the dark ages, in case you haven't noticed?' His disapproval was obvious.

Mishti started pacing up and down the terrace, wringing her hands in agitation, 'Dark ages or not, believe me, I'm caught in a gothic nightmare. I am the mistress of all I survey, yet still a prisoner in my father's castle. You think I don't want to have my way? Settle down with the man of my choice? If only you knew,' she took a deep breath, and resumed her monologue. 'Every time I come close to liking anyone, that person is mercilessly vetted and inspected by my father and his goons. Few people have been able to fulfil the requirements set by my father. Forget about boyfriends, I don't even have proper friends. My father intimidates them all,' she said ruefully. 'The only way to leave this gilded cage is to marry the boy of my father's choice. And frankly speaking, right now, at least visually I am rather appreciative of his taste.'

Pom felt his face heating up as Mishti looked at him with unabashed appreciation. Raja enjoyed his brother's embarrassment; this girl didn't hesitate to speak her mind; but there was a niggling doubt: 'Your father has goons?'

Mishti looked out to the river, 'You guys have no clue, do you? Why do you think your father is so eager to forge a link with my family?

'Palash Bose will be a major political figure in the next local elections, he will be contesting as a candidate for Shyamol Sathi. We all know that he is immensely popular in this region, so odds are that he will definitely win. But Palash Bose knows Raktokarobi will not go gently into the night and fears that the fight will get nasty, which is why he wants my father's henchmen to build up an impenetrable network of intelligence and security around him.

'Don't be taken in by my father's jovial personality,' Mishti continued. 'He hasn't founded his empire by being pleasant to people.' She gestured towards the river, 'Nearly all the traffic on these waters is controlled by my father, he is ruthless in decimating his competitors, and now he has none.

'Palash Bose knows having Girish Sarkar as a close relative will be a significant step towards realizing his electoral aspirations. My dad did a thorough background check on Anupam, and found the boy to his liking. Besides, when Palash Bose becomes the local MLA, Dad would have significant political clout by proxy, and probably turn some of his black money white.'

Mishti scanned the faces of the two brothers, both registering identical levels of surprise and dawning comprehension.

⌁

When confronted with complex problems, Raja would often draw up a game of mental chess, trying to sort out issues on an imaginary chequered board. At that moment, the chessmen skittering around aimlessly in Raja's mind finally synchronized themselves in one fluid movement; he marvelled at his father's astute moves. It was crystal clear why his father had been so desperate to bring Pom down from Kolkata almost at a moment's notice, and why he was bending over backwards to oblige Girish Sarkar.

Arms akimbo, Mishti threw out a challenge to Pom. 'I want to get married as quickly as possible,' she announced like she was the mistress, ethereal yet powerful, of the river that flowed behind her. 'And I do not have any problems in marrying you!'

5

A Long Day's Journey into Night

One month on, Dita, by now reconciled to her fate, was gradually easing into the rhythm of life at Phulpukur College. Commuting back and forth to Salt Lake proved to be a challenge, but since the college did not have a campus, much less inhabitable staff quarters, Dita did not have much of an option. The village itself was riddled with insurmountable economic disparity, most of the populace being indigent farmers, the rest being inexplicably affluent like the Pundit family; there was no golden mean between these extremes.

Dita, however, had managed to make a few friends. Sahana Pundit was Dita's constant companion; despite being a part-time lecturer, Sahana came in almost every day to give Dita support in her ongoing struggles and the teething problems that the college experienced on a regular basis.

Dita met all the other part-time lecturers too, a mixed bag of aspiring teachers who were using their posts in this college as a stopgap before they took up permanent positions of their choice. Some of them were dedicated, others desultory, many of them way too uninterested; but considering the pittance they got as salary from the college, Dita could hardly blame them. She was just thankful that they were there to take the classes. Curiously enough, Tea

Boy seemed to have vanished into thin air, no one seemed to know his whereabouts, even the office staff came up with vague answers when she asked them about him. After some time, she gave up asking. However, a faint uneasiness at the back of her mind refused to go away; she still owed him fuel money.

The students of the college came from a curious cross-section of society; some of them were inhabitants of Phulpukur, sons and daughters of local farmers and hence first-generation literates. Several youngsters came in from neighbouring districts because of their lower-than-average scores in the state-level board exams. Some of them seemed more interested in student politics than in their studies. Dita was amazed to find them strutting around with party flags, chanting slogans, and generally having a gala time outside their classrooms. She therefore found it puzzling that the few lessons of Compulsory English that she taught were packed with enthusiastic students.

She found out later that most of the students did not understand a single word of what she said; they came to see her, wondering about her apparently outlandish accent, the way she talked and effortlessly engaged the class. A few deluded pupils had begun circulating a petition—which was apparently being signed by many an eager student—requesting her to conduct the Compulsory English class in Bengali. Dita refused to be shocked any more, or so she thought!

Dita's phone buzzed. Tamali was on the line. 'Yes, Mom,' she responded absent-mindedly as she looked out of the tiny window of her office and saw many of the students huddled together in clusters and talking animatedly. Something was afoot in the student community.

'Dita,' her mother's insistent voice finally secured her attention. 'I need a favour, darling. Bob Banerjee, the director of the web series I'm currently working on, wants to shoot on location and is on the lookout for a village college campus. I thought I'd check with you. What do you think, would your college campus be a viable option? Bob is not in a hurry, he is busy wrapping up the previous sequences and will be able to start shooting on location in a couple of months' time.'

Dita bit her bottom lip, trying to figure out the risk factor: the new college building was well under way, the ground and first floors were ready; she hoped that the boundary walls and the road leading to the main entrance would soon be ready too. Having the new campus as a location for a web series might be good publicity for the college. She said a tentative 'yes' to her mother and tried to hang up.

Tamali, however, was in the mood to talk. 'Dita, turn on the television if you have one in your office. Phulpukur is being mentioned on quite a few channels.'

Dita was all ears now. 'That's strange! Phulpukur is just a sleepy little village, why is it in the news?'

'Someone from Phulpukur has won the Aeroflot Open Chess Tournament,' Tamali said, her excitement evident in her voice, accompanied by the musical tinkle of her bangles. 'Reports are coming in from Moscow, it's an Indian guy, Anuraj Bose, and they're saying he is originally from Phulpukur village.'

'Oh, I haven't heard anything about it, Mom. I'll have to ask around, I guess,' Dita said, rapidly losing interest as she heard a couple of boys quarrelling outside her window. 'Mom, I have to go now,' Dita hung up and rushed out of her office.

Alok, Praloy, and Sahana were already in the middle of the squabble, trying to stop the boys from beating each other up. A small crowd had gathered around them. Dita was at an utter loss as to how to handle the situation. Suddenly, a stentorian voice rose above the noisy altercation, 'Stop immediately! I will not allow such hooliganism on my campus. Break it up, guys!'

The rowdy crowd parted like the Red Sea before Moses as Devdutt, the headmaster of Saint James, made his way to the centre. 'If you have any problem to be sorted out, please choose your representatives and approach Principal ma'am in a civilized way. No sensible resolution ever came out of creating unnecessary chaos.'

The altercation, as it turned out, was between the student members of Shyamol Sathi and Raktokarobi. Both parties were campaigning to get signatures for the petition against Compulsory English classes and trying to strong-arm anyone they could find to sign the document.

Two belligerent-looking boys followed Dita to her office. She was relieved to see Devdutt had followed her too, hopefully, to guide her through this problematic situation.

Once inside the office, Devdutt glanced angrily at one of the boys. 'What is this commotion all about, Rajeev? I thought I had made it clear to you that you have to keep your politics out of this campus! Haven't I reminded you time and again that this is a school campus on which your college has been given some temporary space? My students are young, they are just children, I do not want them to be corrupted with your petty party politics! Why is this so difficult to understand?'

Refusing to be cowed down by authority, Rajeev retorted belligerently, 'I don't understand why you are yelling only at me, sir?' Impatiently brushing back his greasy hair with one hand he pointed at the other boy, 'He is equally to blame.'

Sighing exasperatedly, Devdutt tried to explain the dynamics of the situation to Dita. 'Rajeev is the student leader of Shyamol Sathi.' Pointing a disapproving finger at the other ruffian, a tall dark boy dressed in a grimy red T-shirt and shabby jeans, he added, 'That is Utpal, the representative for Raktokarobi. Believe it or not, they are fighting over who can gather the greatest number of signatures to make you speak in Bengali for the Compulsory English classes.'

The ludicrous situation reminded Dita of the fight between the Big-Endians and Little-Endians in *Gulliver's Travels*, the two factions who fought against each other in the land of the Lilliput to resolve which end of an egg should be broken first. The solution, in this case, was not too difficult to find. 'According to the statutes of the University of Calcutta, it is compulsory for a lecturer to conduct Compulsory English classes in English. If you have any problem in following the classes, I suggest you use Google Translate,' Dita declared confidently.

And that was that.

Devdutt appeared pleased with the verdict; Sahana and Alok, who had also trooped into the office to see how matters were going, seemed relieved.

The boys left, but they did not appear even remotely convinced about the outcome. They were genuinely perplexed: didn't this woman know that in a village where it is a challenge to ensure two square meals a day, having access to Wi-Fi was a pipe dream, leave alone Google Translate!

Ignoring the disgruntled students, Devdutt left with a word of caution to Dita, 'It's good that you were so firm, the more you seek to pacify them, the more it goes to their heads.'

'Let's go and grab a bite from the canteen,' Sahana suggested, as the hullabaloo died down. 'Even a lukewarm cup of coffee would be welcome.'

'Whew! What a day,' agreed Dita, as she gladly joined Sahana for coffee.

The day, however, was still not done. Palash Bose's call came in around 2 p.m. He got straight to the point, 'I just found out that some boys from Raktokarobi have hoisted the national flag at our college construction site along with their own party banner.'

Dita was stunned. According to her understanding, in India, the national flag could be hoisted on Republic Day or Independence Day, and both those events had long since passed. Why would someone want to hoist the national flag so summarily?

Palash seemed to have read her thoughts, rather uncannily. 'You cannot hoist the flag any day that you wish to,' he stated.

'What is to be done now?' Dita asked, her forehead furrowed in consternation.

'Obviously the flag has to be taken down. But the snag is that no one associated with the college can do it,' a note of worry crept into Palash's voice. 'The Raktokarobi fanatics and their leader Arshad Ali have played their hand well; no matter who brings the flag down, they are going to cry foul and rake up the fight against Shyamol Sathi. They are also going to blame you for supporting Shyamol Sathi.'

Dita couldn't believe her ears. 'I have been as neutral as possible. Why would they blame me?'

'The way I see it, it would have been sensible for you to agree with Rajeev. At the very least, Shyamol Sathi would have been able to give you some protection. Now you have to deal with Arshad Ali and his skewed brand of politics.'

The wily old man knew all about the recent altercation, it seemed. 'So what do I do now?' Dita asked dully.

'Register a complaint with the local police; they will come and take the flag down. No one will be able to complain if the police step in,' came the shrewd advice.

Trying to clear the cobwebs of confusion from her mind, Dita decided to seek help from the office staff. 'I need the phone number of the local police station, please.'

Alok had the number saved on his phone but hesitated before forwarding it to her. 'Calling this number to register your complaint will not help you, ma'am; you have to go physically to the police station, they will need your signature to file the complaint.'

Oh dear, this does not bode well, Dita thought. 'How far is the local police station?'

'Ma'am, there is no local police station in Phulpukur,' Alok could not hide his distress. 'The nearest one is in Diamond Harbour.'

'That's more than half an hour's drive from here,' said Sahana, who had come to sign the attendance book after her classes before heading home. Sympathizing with Dita's plight, the two women tried to find a solution to the mess. But there was simply no way out. Dita would have to go to the Diamond Harbour police station.

Sahana did the next best thing that she could, she called Pinku, explained the situation, adding that she could not let Dita go to a police station all by herself, so she would be accompanying her. Pinku said he would join them in fifteen minutes and would drive them down to Diamond Harbour.

'Sahana, I have to drive back to Kolkata, so I think it would be best that we take my car,' Dita suggested, as they picked up their bags and walked towards the campus gate. Alok followed them, having put in several official documents in his bag, in case the police wanted some proof that the newly constructed building actually belonged to the college. Dita gave Alok a weary but grateful smile when she saw that he was determined to accompany them.

Pinku was already there when they arrived at the gate, but he was not alone. Lo and behold, Tea Boy was there with him. A tenuous, barely-there thread of happiness seemed to wrap itself around Dita's heart. He looks a bit different, Dita thought, and then realized that he was better dressed than he had been on the day that she first met him. The grey eyes were just as attractive though, Dita observed, as a smile lit up his eyes.

'The prodigal son returns, from who knows where!' Dita smiled back. 'You are not a tea boy, I assume?'

'Nah,' he continued smiling, 'I'm Raja.'

'Huh! That hardly explains things,' scoffed Sahana. 'I see you are back!'

'He's back with a bang, don't you think?' Pinku cast an admiring look at Raja as they all got into Dita's car. There was a slight delay as Raja struggled to get into the driver's seat, positioned to accommodate a much shorter person. After making the necessary adjustments, Pinku slid in beside Raja, with Alok and the two ladies in the back seat.

From the easy banter that flowed between Raja, Pinku, and Sahana, it was apparent that they were close friends. Dita sat back and enjoyed their comfortable camaraderie. She still did not know where Raja had come back from but decided she had way too many things to worry about now and was sure she would find out eventually.

They received a royal welcome at the Diamond Harbour police station. Everyone seemed to know Pinku, both because of his family name and his political affiliations. Filing the case was a breeze, with the officer-in-charge of the station himself volunteering to go down to Phulpukur to solve the problem regarding the flag. From a distant corner of her exhausted mind, Dita observed that Raja was also receiving treatment bordering on the obsequious from the police force. I wonder why? she asked herself.

They left the police station with the officer in tow. The man not only gave Dita his phone number and told her to call him in case of any student related disturbances, but also volunteered to take them down to the riverbank. 'Now that you are here, you must see the river Hooghly. My man will guide you to a beautiful stretch, it's not even a five-minute walk from here,' he insisted.

Dita glanced at her watch. 'It's already very late and I have to return to Kolkata. I don't like driving in the dark on the highways, the headlights of oncoming traffic can be quite blinding,' she mumbled.

She must have missed some silent communication between Pinku and Raja, so was rather surprised when Pinku said, 'Raja is headed towards Kolkata today, he can drive you back, perhaps? Meanwhile, you can relax for a bit by the river?'

'Why is he going to Kolkata?' Dita asked stupidly.

'I have a brother up there whom I have not met for a long time now,' offered Raja.

'Don't I know it! For you two even a month is a long time, go and catch up and give him my love,' Pinku said as Sahana and he began walking towards the river.

Dita and Raja followed. The river flowed at its own timeless pace, the waves lapping gently at their feet as they settled down on the sandy banks. As Dita raised her face to take a deep breath, her pert little nose taking in the fresh air that surrounded her, the fatigue and frustration of the day seeped out of her body. She was glad that she had come down to the river and she was glad she had Tea Boy by her side.

Raja could not help but think that Pom would have been enthralled by the beauty of the moment—the turquoise waters of the river, the cool evening breeze, and a bright and intelligent woman for company—Pom would be happy to spend hours in this ecstatic moment. But Raja being Raja was always ready to go a step further, explore uncharted territories, immerse himself into that instant in the wind, liven up each breath, break through all probable boundaries.

Noting the rapt attention with which Dita was looking out at the river, Raja pointed out the various kinds of boats on the flowing waters. 'It's rather interesting, you know, the boat builders of Bengal rarely have any formal education, they make these vessels simply by visually guessing the specifications. Unfortunately, as the demand for such boats has gone down, it is a nearly extinct skill now.' Indicating a couple of boats bobbing up and down ahead of them, Raja continued, 'Those are patia boats, small fishing vessels that can be carried back on the fisherman's shoulders and left to dry out on the beach once the fishing is over.'

Raja's innate knowledge of the topography of the land surprised Dita, as did his attempt to draw her into a comprehensive explanation of the rhythms of the river and the men who rode the waves.

Raja waved at a passing boat, the boatman waved back. 'This is a khorokisti, its name originates from the Persian word kasti, though the Persian connection to riverine Bengal remains unclear to me.' While Raja was talking, the boat had drawn near and Dita was taken by surprise when Raja jumped on to the boat, reached out to her and effortlessly pulled her on to it.

The mahogany-skinned boatman beamed at Raja, obviously happy to see him. 'It seems like ages since I saw you last; just before you went away to Kolkata. You are so tall now, taller than your father, I think. Have you come back to Phulpukur?'

'No, Dhiren kaka, I am here only for a few days,' Raja replied, looking out at the river. 'It's not very easy to live with my father, you know,' he added, giving Dhiren a frank look.

Dhiren chuckled, 'Troubles haven't changed over the years I see!' He recalled an occasion when he had taken Raja back to Phulpukur after one of his attempts to run away from home. The errant boy had hidden on a boat laden with hay and managed to sail quite far before he was found.

And now that unmanageable boy has grown up into a personable young man, and has such a winsome woman in tow, Dhiren observed. He turned away from them, rowing the boat, humming a Bhatiali tune as he edged his vessel downstream.

Gliding back into the waters of the Bhagirathi–Hooghly, the river turned choppy and Dita nearly lost her balance as she tried to sit down in the narrow confines of the boat. Raja reached out immediately, protective arms holding on to her and drawing her into comfortable companionship. Grey eyes twinkled down at her, washing away her fears and inhibitions in a warm tide of inexplicable emotions.

Doe-eyed and vulnerable, Raja echoed Pom's thoughts; the doe eyes were pinning him down, waiting for a response as she cast her spell around him. 'So who are you, Raja, when do I get to know what every boatman in this locality obviously knows?'

Captivated by her eyes and clutching at straws, Raja mumbled, 'Ask me no questions and I'll tell you no lies.'

To hell with Pom, was Raja's last conscious thought before he dipped his head, capturing tender lips in a passionate kiss; behind them the river sparkled in the evening breeze, the world melted away.

6

Sons and Lovers

*P*om's studio apartment in South Kolkata was tiny, just good enough to function as a bachelor pad. It was on the thirtieth floor of a high rise, and the brothers nursed frosted glasses of ice-cold beer as they looked down at the sprawling cityscape. Night had descended, the city lights were dimming, what remained were the flashing reds of the traffic lights.

'It was as if I was kissing her by proxy. I looked at her and could not erase the idea that she was exactly as you had described, all doe-eyed and vulnerable, and I just couldn't resist,' Raja's voice resonated in the silent room.

'I don't know what's wrong with me,' Raja continued, throwing Pom a desperate glance. 'I knew you like her.' He appeared to be struggling with his emotions, caught between his unconditional love for his brother and the desperation of a moment of desire which had caught him unguarded, a moment that had crept up unbidden and engulfed every other conscious thought.

Pom felt a deep tide of sympathy flowing out towards his brother, a young man who was struggling to control his emotions and obviously failing abjectly. He had never seen Raja so unsure of himself; his rogue of a brother was usually brash and confident, and Pom desperately wanted to ease the situation.

'Oh! So now I have to challenge you to a duel, do I? Since you have well and truly stolen my girl from right under my nose?' Pom teased. 'Name your weapon, boy, I will meet you on the banks of the Bhagirathi–Hooghly at daybreak tomorrow.

'On second thoughts, let me have my lance, while you can have your drumsticks,' Pom laughed.

'That's the best choice ever,' Raja's bear hug almost threatened to suffocate Pom. 'Where have you ordered the drumsticks from?'

'Stop manhandling me, Raja, you need not choke me to death,' Pom was struggling for breath when Raja released him with some contrition. 'The drumsticks will come from Mainland China,' he panted, landing a playful smack on Raja's cheek.

'Only drumsticks?' Raja appeared disappointed.

'No, you glutton,' Pom teased. 'Don't I know you? You will want the whole works! I've ordered dim sums, Szechuan fried rice, chilli chicken, and pepper crab, with darsan and vanilla ice cream for dessert.' Raja's happy face was all the answer Pom needed, 'I see it suits your style,' he chuckled.

'Baba would have been over the moon with Kolkata-style Chinese food; he hates mom's dal–roti, rajma–chawal menu!' Raja said.

'What did he have to say about you winning the Aeroflot Open? Was he happy when you came back?' Pom was curious, he had missed this part of the family drama as he had been unable to go down to Phulpukur for the last few weekends.

'He was happy enough with the prize money. I think

by now he has figured out that sometimes there is good money in this game, and it brings you a bit of international recognition too. Otherwise, he is rather ambivalent,' Raja sounded thoughtful. 'I thought I was still getting cold vibes,' he paused, before adding, 'you should have seen mom, she had called half of Phulpukur for lunch to celebrate; people were still busy eating when I stepped out to meet Papu and Pinku.'

'The reason for those cold vibes is not very difficult to figure out, Raja,' Pom swilled his beer. 'At this moment Baba is eminently confused; in the animal kingdom, a confused creature is also a cornered beast and behaves arbitrarily because he cannot really figure out the right way forward. Baba, as is evident to all and sundry, is too energetic a man to sit at home after retirement. Being the president of the governing body of Phulpukur College is a stopgap at best; his real ambition lies in politics, and he wants to make an impressive entry into the political arena of West Bengal.'

Pom stopped to answer the doorbell, the food had arrived. The brothers set the food on the table, sniffing appreciatively as oriental aromas drifted across the room. Pom continued, 'Baba had a heavy-duty strategy in place, being the president of the governing body ensures that he has the complete allegiance of the student members of Shyamol Sathi; the office staff too, in case you haven't noticed, are leaning towards the same. His next step was to secure a reliable ally, this is where Girish Sarkar comes in; Baba thought he had a reasonably good plan up his sleeve, offering me as a match for Mishti.'

'I thought you quite liked Mishti, so where's the snag?' Raja was curious.

Pom's eyebrows shot up, 'And here I thought you were the one who was waxing eloquent about Mishti.'

Raja nearly choked on his food, 'When did I give that impression?'

Pom sighed at his imprudent brother, 'The other day on the terrace of her house, you were literally gushing your approval of the girl!'

'Fuck you, Pom. Mishti was ready to eat out of your hands,' Raja tittered. 'I've not spared a single thought for Mishti in the last one month. And if I remember correctly, she was very vocal in her desire to marry you! You were her eye candy; where do I feature in all of this? Seriously, get a grip, bro!'

'Fuck you too, bro,' countered Pom. 'Because Baba has somehow latched on to the idea that Mishti prefers you to me, and since I stipulated that I need a few months to mull over whether I want to get married or not, I think his suspicions have assumed the shape of indisputable facts! He thinks I am just covering up for your absence, and that I am waiting for you to return and clear it up with Mishti! He now considers you to be the root of all evil.

'What is more, he is unsure of the dynamics between Papu and you,' Pom continued with wicked glee. 'The way the two of you were hugging each other that day has set him thinking!'

Raja was rendered speechless. Taking advantage of the failure of his brother's vocal cords, Pom positioned his hypothesis adroitly, 'Look at the entire fiasco from Baba's point of view now, Raja, and you will understand why he is upset. You sabotaged his first meeting with Dita Roy, you gave off ambivalent signals regarding Girish's daughter, and you have fed him the idea that I like Dita Roy! The fallout is that Mishti wants to marry you, but you are quite happy in the comfort of Papu's embrace.'

The chessmen in Raja's mind whizzed out of control. 'I need a stiff drink,' he groaned. 'This beer isn't helping.'

'This is a minefield of your own making, and now that things are getting out of hand, you cannot sit back and complain. No options now, Raja, we actually have to fight it out,' Pom sounded dead serious. 'I think you are exacerbating the situation by not revealing your identity to Dita, she might not take it well when she realizes that you are the son of someone whom she considers to be her arch-enemy nowadays.'

'Pom, that is exactly why I can't tell her, at least not now; I don't want her to think any less of me because of the mutual animosity between Baba and her.' Raja appeared to be weary of it all. 'It's maddening,' he sighed.

They finished their meal in companionable silence, then stretched out in front of the huge television screen on the wall to dig into the darsan and ice cream.

'I felt so proud when they carried the news of you winning the championship, it was on several channels, but there were no video clips, they just mentioned your name,' Pom was well aware of Raja's reticence to be in the limelight.

'It is not as if people are dying to learn about chess championships across the world; it is not as if it is cricket or football, with a whopping fan following. Chess has a very limited number of aficionados, so no one was really complaining too much when I refused to give interviews. I just want to lie low for some time,' Raja explained. 'This world is too much with us.'

'Wordsworth,' observed Pom. 'You and your love of the English bards, maybe you should have studied literature.'

'Maybe that is why I find Dita so attractive,' Raja mused. 'Who knows?'

'Was it only that one kiss by the river?' Pom was curious. 'You drove her back home, right?'

'I drove her back home, but there was very little conversation on the way back. She fell asleep on my shoulder. Methinks I have a frozen shoulder,' Raja laughed.

'Baba led her a merry dance today,' Raja shared his concern with Pom. 'Unrest among the students regarding her classes, and then the mindless nonsense about some flag-hoisting issue; poor soul, by the time we were ready to drive back, she was thoroughly exhausted.... Anyway, what's the status between you and Mishti now?'

Pom groaned, 'That girl is driving me nuts, Raja. She refuses to take no for an answer. I don't have any issues against her, as such, but I have serious reservations about marrying the daughter of some random mafioso, because at the end of the day that is what Girish Sarkar is.

'She is stalking me on social media, she has managed to get my phone number, and to beat it all she barged in on me here, in my apartment, a week ago.'

'You don't say!' Raja was taken aback that Mishti could be so intrusive.

'She used the pretext of wanting to see the apartment she was expected to settle in, once she married me,' Pom's voice reflected his amazement at Mishti's audacity. 'She was completely sure that I would eventually say yes to the marriage; that it was just a matter of time before I agreed.'

Pom looked at Raja and lowered his voice to a mock

whisper, 'I did the only thing I could to extricate myself from this hopeless situation.'

'What did you do, Pom? What did you do?' Raja asked with trepidation.

'I said I was in love with Dita Roy and I wanted to marry her!'

The two brothers looked at each other for one long moment before bursting into raucous and unholy laughter.

7

The Winter's Tale

December arrived; the harsh rays of the summer sun gave way to the weak light of winter; the denizens of Phulpukur heaved a sigh of relief as the days became noticeably cooler; they drew out their musty blankets, and aired them in the sun, and prepared themselves for the long winter nights. Anticipation hung in the air, the inaugural day of the Phulpukur College campus was drawing near.

Biltu, the office boy, had been run off his feet, sprinting from pillar to post on a hundred errands: distributing pamphlets announcing the inauguration across the village, organizing refreshments for the invitees, and placing orders with the village florist for garlands and bouquets of fresh flowers that would be required to welcome the dignitaries on the big day.

Alok, Praloy, and Ashok spent sleepless nights arranging funds for the occasion and dancing to the whims of the members of the governing body, all of whom had different requests to be fulfilled. Even the normally docile Pinku and Papu suddenly metamorphosed into intractable monsters, throwing tantrums if their demands were not met instantly.

Palash Bose, as usual, revelled in his role of the chorus leader, orchestrating moves, reaching out to the crème de la crème of Shyamol Sathi in Kolkata, and driving everybody crazy with his mood swings. Dita tried to steer clear as much as she could, but nonetheless became the target of his blistering comments once too often. The man had the nerve to tell Dita not to wear high heels on the day of the inauguration, as they would be undertaking a token march from the school campus to that of the college. He also asked her not to wear her sunglasses—they were too fashionable, he opined, and made her look totally out of place in Phulpukur. To top it all, he also suggested that it would actually be convenient for her if she settled down somewhere in Phulpukur village: she would be able to devote more time to matters of college administration and also save on the fuel she was burning regularly, driving up and down from Salt Lake. Dita could hardly control her irritation, but dismissed his meddling as the idiosyncrasy of an opinionated patriarch.

To make matters worse, Raja had pulled a disappearing trick on her, vanishing into thin air after the evening he drove her to Kolkata. She realized she still did not have his phone number and was too embarrassed to ask Sahana for it. Unable to forget their passionate embrace, she felt embarrassed that she didn't even know his full name and felt too awkward to ask her colleagues about him, in case her queries gave rise to unnecessary gossip. She seriously wondered if there was any point in investing time to even think about that errant young man. On a couple of occasions, she had overheard Palash ranting and raving on his phone and Raja's name seemed to come up repeatedly during those conversations. At such times, Dita felt glad that Raja could irritate Palash to that extent, and was almost ready to forgive him for his lapses.

Palash Bose had no one to share his misery with: even Hemlata turned a deaf ear to his complaints. Nowadays, she thought, there were too many of them and left him to his devices. Over the last few months, Girish had repeatedly called him to enquire about the status of the marriage proposal between the two families. Palash tried to take as much evasive action as possible, often going to the extent of ignoring his calls, until one day Girish came over to the Bose household and dropped the bombshell that Pom had conveyed to Mishti that he did not want to marry her. Apparently, he was in love with Dita Roy.

Palash was rendered speechless with fury. What had he done to deserve two such stubborn sons?

Hemlata bore the brunt of his anger for having given birth to two ungrateful brats, neither of whom were willing to help and support Palash when he really needed them. A frustrated and furious father was to be avoided at all costs; hence Pom refused to budge from Kolkata, summarily ignoring Palash's calls. Palash realized that he had to fix the situation with Girish, and fix it real soon, before Girish washed his hands of Palash's plans.

In sheer desperation, he decided to call Raja, who was in Tamil Nadu, attending the ONGC Chess Championship. The conversation between the father and son was so very heated, that it was almost combustible.

Raja had just wrapped up a long drawn-out and rather tense game when his phone began to buzz. It was his father on the line. Raja frowned; his father did not call him often; a frisson of worry ran through his mind as he answered the call.

Palash did not believe in opening a conversation with formal niceties, so he came straight to the point. 'Raja, I need you to drill some sense into Pom, the stupid boy is refusing to marry Mishti.'

'But surely that is Pom's prerogative, Baba, how can I convince him otherwise?' Raja demurred.

'You two are thick as thieves, Raja,' Palash barked into the phone. 'If anyone can convince him, it is you.'

'Why would I want to convince him, Baba? If he does not want to marry Mishti, it is his decision. And I fail to understand why you want to dictate terms in his life. It is high time you accept the right of individual choices and stop trying to control him.'

Palash struggled to rein in his temper. 'Next you will also tell me, I suppose, that you know about his plans to marry Dita Roy? That chit of a girl, I can't fathom when or where she keeps meeting your brother to wring out such undying protestations of love and commitment!'

Raja was dumbfounded. Rumours are like Chinese whispers, he realized, each person adds his own bit of information to them before passing them on. The rumour-mongers were obviously having a field day in Phulpukur: the next thing he was likely to hear about was the happy couple's honeymoon destination.

Suppressing a laugh, Raja muttered, 'That is also his choice, Baba. If he wants to marry Dita Roy, and Dita Roy wants to marry him, who are we to stop them?'

'It will be equivalent to hara-kiri for the entire family, Raja. Girish Sarkar will not take rejection kindly,' Palash yelled.

'But surely you can't ask Pom to sacrifice his happiness

for the benefit of the family, or more particularly your benefit, Baba? The way I see it don't *you* stand to gain the most from this alliance with Girish Sarkar?'

Livid with anger, Palash lowered his voice to a threatening whisper. 'Since you are so very concerned about your brother's well-being, I will not stand against him if he really wants to marry Dita Roy.

'Mishti, however, will marry into our family! Girish has suggested that if it is not Pom, then it has to be you, Raja! I hope you understand the consequences of denying Girish. Now it's not even a choice, it's a fait accompli!'

This time it was Raja who screamed into the resounding silence—the desperate cry of a terrified man who is about to be hung, drawn, and quartered.

8

Wolf Hall

As the short winter days dissolved into the somnolence of long, gloomy nights, Dita found herself struggling to reach home before dark; on some days, she would get caught up in mindless governing body meetings after the normal college schedule and found it difficult to drive back to Kolkata in those late hours. Long stretches of the highway were devoid of adequate street lighting, and she often drove through miles and miles of complete darkness lit up only by the headlights of the passing traffic.

On one such evening, Dita's car screeched to a halt as a wild animal leapt out of the dense vegetation which surrounded Phulpukur, just before the village road merged into the highway. Her heart racing from the shock, Dita cautiously observed the creature standing just a foot away from her car's front bumper. It had short and fuzzy greyish red fur with grey undertones and a distinct dark V-shaped patch on its shoulders. Its limbs, Dita noticed, were paler than its body. Its eyes glistened like gemstones, reflecting the brilliance of the car's headlights and Dita could just about discern a feral howl as it looked at her car with savage irritation. Dita waited with mounting trepidation, praying that the animal would not come any closer. After what seemed like ages, it slunk away into the darkness of a nearby grove. Dita heaved a sigh of relief and drove on.

The following day, Dita reached the college late only to find a small crowd in her office, conversing in hushed tones and nodding in approval at the central attraction in the room. This was a huge rosewood table topped with a flawless piece of frosted glass around which the crowd had gathered. Dita smirked. The table was a marked improvement over the rickety plastic table which had adorned her office on the school campus. She had personally gone and placed orders for college furniture after they received a small furniture grant from the government; her petitions and letters to the authorities were obviously bearing fruit for the college.

It was no mean achievement to detect a glimmer of appreciation in Palash's eyes too, thought Dita. Just before his face took on his habitual shuttered look, he turned around to introduce the two men who were standing next to him. 'This is Aditya Pundit, the son of the founding father of our college; he was here on the day of the inauguration but wasn't able to meet you in all that crowd; and this is Girish Sarkar, a businessman and very dear friend of mine.'

'This is a very handsome table, I must say,' Palash remarked as Dita asked everyone to take a seat, still unsure as to why so many people had gathered in her room today. Displaying yet again the rather eerie habit of reading her thoughts, Palash smiled, 'No, we did not meet here to marvel at your newest acquisition; I called everyone gathered here on an emergency basis because Phulpukur is facing an unanticipated challenge—wolf attacks.'

Murmurs of excited conversations broke out as the staff and teachers present in the room began narrating their harrowing experiences with the stray wolf.

Aditya Pundit took charge. There was something in his demeanour that made everyone sit up and pay attention to him: after all, he was the son of an erstwhile dacoit, and one of the most famous hunters in the region.

'Going by the description of this creature, it appears to be an Indian wolf,' he explained. 'In general, this species is to be found in regions of red soil in and around West Midnapore. Typically, wolves do not cover great distances, I cannot really figure out how it got here; but one reassuring thought is that these animals do not turn aggressive until and unless they are attacked or they are injured.'

'Aditya, the problem is that *we* know the nature of the Indian wolf, but unfortunately the villagers in this region do not. Just the sight of the wolf is making them panic,' Girish stated. 'We cannot expect any rational behaviour on their part; for all we know they may gather together and start chasing the wolf with sticks and stones, creating utter confusion and chaos.'

'Which is precisely why I want to take pre-emptive action,' Aditya declared. 'Let's organize a small search party and scan the areas in which the wolf was seen, starting from the place of its last sighting.'

Everyone nodded in approval. Dita decided to speak up. 'Actually, I think I saw it last night. I was driving back to Kolkata, and this creature crossed the road right in front of me, just as I was about to merge onto the highway.'

Another buzz of excited conversation washed across the room. 'How do we know that it's a lone wolf and not an entire pack?' Dipten, the librarian, sounded anxious.

Aditya Pundit tried to reassure him, 'The Indian wolf rarely moves in packs,' but Dipten did not appear even remotely convinced.

Girish lent his support to Aditya, 'It's only a wolf, no need to worry so much. Both Aditya and I are licensed hunters. We will have our guns with us, just to be safe.'

'Pinku and Papu will be joining you,' said Sahana. 'Both of them are licensed hunters too.'

'It's decided, then. Let's set out in an hour's time. We have a vast stretch of land to survey,' Aditya said as he stood up to leave.

'Perhaps I can help you there, since I think I am the last person to have spotted it. It makes sense for me to accompany you,' Dita offered tentatively.

Aditya was impressed. The young woman was intelligent and brave, a tad foolhardy maybe, but he was pleased with her offer to help. It would make the tracking easier for them. He nodded his approval.

Palash refused to be excluded from the search party. As they stepped out of the room, he whispered to Girish, 'I am not a hunter, but I want to come along. If you can take that silly girl, you can take me too. The only snag is that I don't have a gun.'

Girish laughed and whispered, 'I will lend you a shotgun, don't worry.' Indicating Dita he said, 'You have a formidable adversary, Palash. That is no silly girl. No wonder she has managed to bewitch Pom.'

Palash Bose had no rejoinder to that.

⌒

The small group of hunters trooped to Aditya's house, where Papu and Pinku were waiting for them. So was Radha, ready with a quintessential Bong lunch of rice, dal, vegetables, and fish curry to fortify them before they embarked on the wolf trail. Personally, she was convinced that the wolf must have crossed the border by now and migrated to Bangladesh.

While they were eating, Palash called Hemlata to let her know he might be late getting back home today. It was Friday, and Pom had driven down for the weekend and Raja was back from Tamil Nadu. Palash was expecting a full house for dinner tonight.

Hemlata, however, was taken aback, 'Why do you want to go wolf tracking? You know nothing about tracking, and at your age it might be an unnecessary risk.' Her sons were talking animatedly in the background, so she appealed to them. 'Guys, your father is going off to chase a wolf! I think he has gone mad, you should try and stop him.'

Palash could hardly keep the frustration out of his voice. 'Stop being so dramatic, Hemlata, it's not a man-eating tiger that we are chasing; even that clueless girl, Dita, is part of the group and no one is banging their heads over that,' he scolded.

'What? Dita must be as insane as you!' Hemlata was at her wits' end. 'Why would she want to join a tracking party? It makes no sense,' she huffed. By now, she had the complete attention of her sons, two pairs of grey eyes were looking at her with an expression which can only be described as horror.

꜀

It was midday when the search party finally started out. Dita guided Girish's massive SUV to the spot where she had encountered the animal the previous evening. The men trooped out of the car and vanished into the dense vegetation that overhung on both sides of the road. Even Jai, the driver, crept out to join the fray after instructing her not to leave the vehicle.

Dita sat and waited, and waited, and waited some more. Because it was winter, Jai hadn't switched on the air conditioner of the car, and Dita began to feel claustrophobic as the inside of the vehicle heated up gradually. Irritated and cross for having voluntarily landed herself in this situation, she ignored the tiny voice of concern that whispered tentative warnings and stepped out. The air outside was fresh and pure with a hint of chill. Feeling somewhat relaxed at last, she pulled out her AirPods and plugged into her favourite music. That animal will surely not cross the same road twice in such a short interval, she reasoned; but then she had totally discounted Murphy's most essential law: anything that can go wrong, will go wrong.

Standing there, all alone in the winter sun, Dita realized she was bone-weary. The last few months of driving up and down from Salt Lake to Phulpukur—with the added pressure of being constantly exposed to unimaginable challenges on a daily basis and Palash Bose's unexplained hostility—were dragging her down. She wondered whether it was worth continuing with this struggle. Billie Eilish crooned into her ears.

The lyrics of 'Lovely' resonated through her body, easing unreconciled frustrations, making her feel drowsy.

A sudden movement caught her eye. Half asleep she stepped into the shadows of the trees, the 'Lovely' songstress urging her on.

By the time the song ended, she had ventured deep into

the undergrowth, surrounded by ancient trees shrouded with emerald green moss and a few butterflies fluttering around flowers that had bloomed out of season. Dita looked back, but she could not see the road any more.

Plugging out the music, she dialled Sahana's number. 'I think I'm lost,' she confessed in an expressionless voice. She heard a gasp at the other end; Sahana, who seemed to be a million miles away, was asking her questions which she was unable to answer. She looked around desperately to give Sahana some landmark, but all the trees seemed identical, she did not even know what kind of trees they were. 'Butterflies, I thought you don't see these fragile creatures during winter; but when you do, they signify hope and renewal,' Dita's voice sounded dreamy. 'I can see a great many wings fluttering in the winter sun,' she remarked as she settled down to admire the view. Petrified, Sahana dialled Pinku.

The search party which had gone out hunting for a wolf now started looking for Dita. Girish kept scolding Jai for leaving Dita all alone on the road, as they spread out in pairs to locate her.

By the time Sahana got around to calling Raja, the brothers were already on the road, driving like mad men to join the search party. Sahana mentioned the butterflies that Dita was talking about. 'Give me her phone number,' Raja barked.

Dita was still gazing at the butterflies and their beautiful wings, reconciled to the fact that they would give way in a few hours to the wings of mosquitoes which haunted the winter nights in this area. She was mulling over this morose thought when her phone buzzed: it was an unknown number. On any other day, she would not respond to unknown numbers, but today, because she thought she was lost and had nothing better to do, she responded to the call, mentally expecting it to be some random call centre trying to make her invest in something.

A voice that sounded vaguely familiar broke into her reverie, 'Where exactly are you?' There was an underlying note of panic in that voice.

'Why should I tell you? Besides, even Google Maps can't locate me in this godforsaken wilderness,' she said dismissively.

He hissed his disapproval. 'Dita, be serious; wolf or no wolf, it will be dark soon, we need to track you down before that!'

'But I really cannot give you any specific landmark,' Dita replied, struggling to drag herself out of the lassitude that had settled on her. 'I can only see trees, nothing else,' she muttered.

'Dita, look around you,' the voice on the phone insisted. 'Can you figure out if the trees are a little less dense somewhere?'

Unsure, but trying to follow the instructions of the voice, she walked in the direction in which she thought the trees were thinning out marginally. She took a few steps, stopped, and then walked ahead again. 'I think I can see a small waterbody to my left,' she informed the voice. 'It looks like a lily pond, but there are no blooms.' The voice let out a whoop of delight.

'Dita, there is only one lily pond nearby, keep it to your left and walk straight ahead, you will come to a clearing, wait there, we'll come and get you!'

'Raja,' she croaked. 'Is that you?'

'Who else would be bothered about you, crazy coot that you are!' came the droll reply. 'Wait in the clearing; don't wander off with the butterflies.'

Ending the call, Raja dialled Papu's number. 'You'll find her in the clearing near the chestnut trees. Go get her before she marches off to some undisclosed location.'

Pom eyed Raja quizzically, 'I thought you just promised her that you are going to get her; she will be expecting you!'

'Pom, you are forgetting that Baba will be there too. There's no point in having a family drama out in the open. He already has some seriously wacko ideas in his head, let's not complicate matters.'

Dita waited patiently in the clearing, where the search party finally caught up with her but there was no sign of Raja. Somehow, Dita was not too surprised. At least she had managed to save his number.

9

Much Ado about Nothing

Girish Sarkar magnanimously lent his SUV and driver to drop Dita home. The day's misadventures had taken their toll on her, and she did not have enough strength to complain. In Girish's scheme of things, it is always good to keep your adversaries unaware of your thoughts, study them from close quarters, and wait for an opportunity to strike. He had already marked Dita as a formidable challenge; after meeting her he understood why Pom would choose her over Mishti—not only was she pretty, she was sharp and intelligent, which was evident in the way she was running the college.

Girish's driver Jai returned with plenty of stories about Dita and her family. He had obviously talked incessantly with her while driving her to Kolkata. Girish listened intently as Jai revealed that Dita's father was an archaeologist based in Delhi, holding a prominent position with the Archaeological Survey of India. Because he travelled extensively, Dita's mother had decided to stay in Kolkata rather than have the family gallivanting across the globe at the drop of a hat.

Finally, like a magician pulling a rabbit out of a hat, Jai switched on the television in Girish's study. He flipped through several channels before settling on the popular channel Kolkata Calling, where he excitedly pointed out a character actor in one of its web series. 'That is Tamali Roy, Dita ma'am's mother.' Hands on his cheeks, he settled down on the carpet to gape at her.

'Oh! And Dita ma'am mentioned something else,' Jai remembered. 'She said that Bob Banerjee, the producer–director of most of the web series being aired on Kolkata Calling, will be coming to Phulpukur soon. He wants to shoot on the college campus for a new project that he is working on.'

Girish was impressed with Jai's sleuthing talents. Armed with this latest bit of information, he could not help but appreciate Dita's farsightedness in granting access to the camera crew to film on campus and earn a reputation for the college beyond Phulpukur. He wondered how Palash would react to this information; Dita's decision would definitely undermine Palash yet again. It was Palash's hope that after becoming the local MLA, he would be empowered to build up Phulpukur College's reputation in the state, but Dita's move had pre-empted his ambitions and would bring the college popularity and instantaneous fame.

Personally, Girish was of the opinion that no matter how much Palash wanted to establish himself as the alpha male of the family, his wife and sons clearly had minds of their own. But who was he to complain? Even Mishti was proving to be utterly incorrigible these days. We are nurturing a generation of ungrateful children, he thought ruefully.

∿

These were almost the same thoughts that were playing out in Palash's mind as he dragged his shotgun home; in the mayhem of the hunt for Dita, the group had dispersed chaotically and Palash was unable to return the gun to Girish. As he lugged the deadweight of the unused weapon, he wondered how Papu knew that Dita would be in the clearing. He had very little faith in today's youth. They were always up to mischief, and even Dita appeared to be a dunderhead: why would she want to pull a disappearing trick?

Palash blamed her squarely for having lost the opportunity to track the wolf. While the search team was running around in circles trying to locate Dita, the villagers had spotted the wolf in the vicinity of the Shyamol Sathi Party office; the forest department had received calls of distress from the villagers and intervened with surprising speed to capture the beast and take it away. Apparently, there was some media coverage too, but he had missed it all.

Hemlata was glad that Palash was back in one piece and limped to the kitchen to give instructions to the cook. Palash dragged the gun up to his bedroom and kicked it under the bed, away from prying eyes. Hemlata would throw a fit if she saw him with a gun. He made a mental note to return it to Girish at the earliest possible opportunity. Thankfully, the boys were nowhere to be seen.

A couple of hours later, when the family finally settled down for dinner, Palash broached the topic of Pom's marriage again. 'My harping on and on about this marriage might seem to be an exercise in futility, but since Pom is obviously smitten with Dita....'

'When did Pom meet Dita?' Hemlata was puzzled. 'As far as I know it is you who keeps meeting Dita on a regular basis.'

Raja laughed, 'Ma, are you insinuating that it is Baba who should be smitten, because he interacts more with Dita?'

Hemlata ignored Raja's somewhat irreverent remark. 'Pom, when did you meet Dita?' she asked, pinning Pom down with an irate grey gaze. Pom looked at Raja helplessly: their mother could be worse than the Spanish Inquisition if she wanted to know something!

'I think I met her once or twice in passing,' Pom mumbled.

'And once in a dream too,' Raja's information earned him a kick in the shins under the table.

'Once or twice? Please specify?' Hemlata continued doggedly. 'And what exactly do you mean by "in passing"?'

'I saw her from a distance on the day she joined the college,' Pom replied. 'Another time I met her for a few moments while I was picking up Papu on the way to Diamond Harbour.'

Hemlata's eyebrows shot up in surprise. 'And on the basis of these fleeting encounters you've decided that you want to marry her?'

'The dream encounter was not so fleeting, Ma. Pom took his time with that one,' Raja squealed with pain as Pom kicked him again.

Hemlata's grey eyes clouded over with concern, 'Does Dita know about any of this?'

'No.' Pom was beginning to look distinctly uneasy.

'So, you are basically asking us to believe that you want to marry a girl whom you have met for a few seconds and who may not even be aware of your existence?' Hemlata's face paled with disbelief. 'And obviously she does not know or share your sentiments, that is, if you actually have any sentiments? Who are you kidding, beta?'

'When did I ever tell you that I wanted to marry her?' Pom hedged. 'You guys are just carving out imaginary scenarios; you are not really listening to me.'

Palash was nearly apoplectic now. 'How can you say we are imagining things? You told Mishti that you don't want to marry her.'

'I did tell Mishti that I do not want to marry her. However, this answer was way too straightforward for her; it did not sit well with her ego, she needed a justifiable reason as to why she was being rejected. So, I came up with the best reason that I could think of—I fobbed her off with Dita's name.'

This confession had varied impacts on the listeners. Palash was furious, Hemlata appeared smug that she had been able to wring the truth out of Pom, and Raja's face reflected a devilish glee. 'The name was lodged in his subconscious mind, which is why it slipped so easily off his tongue,' Raja declared. 'Poor unsuspecting Mishti, she does not know that she has to fight it out with an ideal, and not an actual, woman.'

Casting a warning glance at Hemlata, Palash decided to take charge. 'Since Raja is so conscious of the needs of Pom's subconscious mind, let's change the proposed bridegroom for Mishti! Girish himself has expressed his desire to make Raja his son-in-law.'

'But Mishti is neither the ideal nor the actual woman that I would want to marry,' Raja protested. 'Don't I get a say in my own marriage?'

'No,' Palash answered curtly.

Raja turned to Pom and intoned in a stage whisper, 'Did I tell you, I am eloping with Papu? It's all planned.'

Poker-faced, Hemlata asked, 'Does Papu know about your plans?'

10

Pride and Prejudice

No ifs, ands, or buts; Bob Banerjee personified the popular image of the eccentric film director. A head of wild, untameable hair, glasses perpetually positioned on the top of his head, as if to keep his overflowing locks in place rather than being used to improve the clarity of his vision, this wiry and energetic man seemed to picture everything through the perspective of his camera. He did not seem to mind that a sizeable crowd had gathered around them, staring with blatant curiosity at the actors and the crew. Students joined the show whenever they had free classes, some of them hoping that their faces might come up in crowd scenes.

'In another life, he would have been a pirate with his spyglass, Captain Bob on the deck of the *Hispaniola*,' Dita pointed out to Tamali, as mother and daughter stood in the winter sun, watching Bob running around the campus, trying to figure out the perfect spot for his shot.

From the stares that kept coming their way, it was evident that Tamali's was a well-known face on screen; Dita's office staff kept trotting up and down the lawns to meet Tamali and Bob. Not really accustomed to being the centre of attention, Tamali was actually enjoying the moment. Sahana came up with Pinku and Papu, who were so pleased to meet Tamali that they kept insisting that she should visit their home. It was one of the oldest mansions in the village, they explained, as if that would make it a more attractive proposition for her.

From the corner of her eye, Dita saw Alok trying to attract her attention from the front of the office block. What can be amiss now, Dita thought glumly, as she hurried towards the office. As it turned out the hullabaloo was about the Bengali teacher Agni, and his rather objectionable behaviour towards a student named Seema. Angry voices denounced the way in which Agni had repeatedly targeted Seema, asking her to come and sit on the front bench during his classes. If she demurred, Agni would threaten her with the prospect of failing her in his subject. The harassment had been going on for quite a while, until Agni finally revealed his egotistical intentions and proposed marriage to his beleaguered student.

For many months, Agni kept reiterating in his classes that he came from a reasonably affluent family and bragged about the brands of clothes that he wore and the latest versions of phones that he carried. While Seema squirmed, pale and wan, seated at the front of the class, too embarrassed even to make eye contact with her peers, Agni kept extolling his own market value to the girl. Finally, the students in his class decided to take matters into their own hands. Their complaints came in from two justifiable angles: firstly, they were way behind in the syllabus because the lecturer was too busy bragging about his clothes and phones and generally superior lifestyle; secondly, it was painful to see Seema endure such harassment in silence.

'Of course, action must be taken against the errant teacher,' Dita sought to pacify the agitated students. 'Rest assured that we will take appropriate steps to iron out the situation. Go back to your classes; the management will deal with this.'

After the students dispersed, Dita tried to control the rage which bubbled up. 'This is unacceptable behaviour,' she told Alok in an icy tone. 'We need to suspend Agni for at least a few days to set a precedent that such conduct will not be tolerated from any teacher.'

Alok gave an unconvincing nod, while Praloy mumbled, 'Agni is an active member of Shyamol Sathi; it might be difficult to suspend him without inviting the wrath of the party. Besides, he is very close to Palash Bose. A suspension would require the acquiescence of the governing body, and somehow, I don't think its president would agree. It would eventually be a loss of face for you, ma'am.'

Dita refused to be cowed down. 'But if I don't fight back, it will be a loss of face for me with my students.' She picked up her phone and dialled Palash Bose's number.

∿

Palash hurried to the college campus, not wanting Dita to take a unilateral decision which might come back to haunt them later. Girish Sarkar and Mishti, who were visiting Palash, decided to accompany him. Mishti was all agog at the prospect of finally meeting Dita.

Strange sights and sounds greeted them as they entered the campus. An array of cameras rounded off the lawn next to the newly installed canteen; swarms of people were flitting in and out of the area. As the human wall shifted and swayed, Palash spotted a rather wild-looking man gesticulating dramatically. Nonplussed, Palash couldn't help staring.

Girish cleared his throat noisily. 'So I see that Dita has actually managed to get Bob Banerjee down to Phulpukur.'

'Bob who?' Palash asked.

Mishti had already started to run towards the crowd; spotting Papu, she waved excitedly and elbowed her way in to catch a glimpse of the actors. Pinku turned around to see a girl hurtling like a loose cannonball into the crowd. Papu smiled with undiluted pleasure. 'This is Mishti,' he said excitedly, introducing the girl to Pinku.

Unperturbed by his daughter's unequivocal desertion, Girish gestured ruefully towards the crowd, 'Palash, sometimes it makes sense to catch up with popular culture too, you cannot always keep your head buried in books and political manifestos.'

Palash ignored the jibe, as Girish continued, 'Bob Banerjee is a prolific director and producer, almost single-handedly responsible for a spate of super-hit web series that have been rolled out of Kolkata Calling in the last few years. He's as eccentric as they come, but his crew and actors literally worship the ground he walks on.'

Palash seemed rooted to the spot, 'But why is he here? Where did he hear about Phulpukur?'

'Tamali Roy is one of the most sought-after actors in Bob's team,' Girish explained. 'She is Dita's mother. I think Bob was on the lookout for a village campus to shoot a new series and that is how it all happened.'

Palash wondered how Girish knew so much about everything. Keeping an eye on the shenanigans of the crowd, they walked at a leisurely pace towards the college office.

An extremely agitated Agni was waiting for them in Dita's office. Red in the face and quivering with rage, he pounced on Palash and Girish like an infuriated animal being deprived of its prey. 'I simply don't understand why Dita ma'am is lending an ear to such slander. There's not even an iota of truth in these accusations.'

'Sit down and explain exactly what happened,' Palash cut in rather rudely into Agni's rant.

Taken aback by Palash's tone, Agni started mumbling, 'This girl wasn't paying attention in my classes, so I made her sit in the first row. She is a slow learner.... I don't suppose she understood the kind of effort I was really extending to bring her up to scratch.'

'That's not the version that we've heard from the students,' Dita interjected.

Agni flared up again. 'Fabrications, all of them, and all of them politically motivated. If I am not wrong, Seema is dating Utpal, the student leader for Raktokarobi. They have made it part of their agenda to target me because they think I support Shyamol Sathi.'

Palash had very little patience with Agni's histrionics. Wanting to settle the issue as quickly as possible, he asked Alok to get hold of Utpal and Rajeev, the student leaders for the two parties.

Dita looked at Palash, 'You seriously want me to believe that Rajeev hasn't been coached by now to give a political colour to this situation? You people have deadly cabals out there!'

Sure enough, as soon as Utpal and Rajeev entered the room, it became a matter of mudslinging, one political faction against the other. Agni's misdemeanour receded into the background. Rajeev was out to prove that Utpal had cleverly placed his girlfriend as bait to defame Agni and

Shyamol Sathi by extension, while Utpal was hell-bent on proving that Seema was being targeted because she was his girlfriend, and he headed Raktokarobi.

The argument went on endlessly, and Dita realized that all this was just a diversion to let Agni wriggle off the hook. Hers was perhaps the only neutral voice in this sea of chaos, but she was sure that she would be overridden by Palash.

Weary of it all, she asked the boys to wait outside the room to hear the administration's final decision. Heedless of the risks that she was putting herself in, she stated her opinion, 'To me it appears to be a violation of the code of conduct which should exist between an educator and his student. As an educational institution, we need to uphold the idea that any student who walks into our classroom does not feel threatened or harassed by the teacher. Is that not a basic requirement?'

She stopped to gather her thoughts, 'In this case I think Agni should undertake a token suspension at the very least for having instigated some grave concerns in the student community. He needs to take some time off to introspect as to why he has not been able to generate trust and confidence among his students. And he definitely needs to apologize to the girl, we do not want our college to be associated with tales of intimidation rather than enlightenment.'

There was complete silence in the room. Savage, thought Girish, the girl does not pull her punches. This did not go down well with Palash; his face resembled a thundercloud as he fought for control.

When Mishti entered the room with Papu and Pinku, it seemed as if she had stepped into a minefield brimming with hidden explosives ready to go up in flames at the least provocation. At first glance, what Mishti saw was a frozen tableau, in which a waif of a girl was ready to lock horns with the most powerful men in Phulpukur. Let's see if she can hold her ground, thought Mishti.

'On the other hand, if we give in to the unfounded claims of the students and punish a teacher so arbitrarily, are we really sending out the right message?' Palash roared. 'Bear in mind, you are a teacher too. If you set Agni as a precedent, no one knows what charges they will be bringing in next; they might feel empowered enough to challenge you too.'

'We will cross that bridge when we come to it,' Dita said dismissively. To all intents and purposes, these two resembled two pugilists in an arena ready to fight to the death. Neither one of them looked ready to give an inch.

While everyone waited with bated breath for a climactic conclusion, Papu delivered a googly, 'Seema is the third girl, isn't she, that you have proposed marriage to in this college, Agni?' he asked innocently. 'The younger the better, it seems,' he winked melodramatically at the flabbergasted Agni.

Dita had primed herself for the final showdown with Palash, and in that battle-ready state, Papu's words took a whole minute to sink in. An alien and unexpected response reared its mischievous head somewhere deep within her soul, one bubble followed another, light, effervescent, yet insistent. To everyone's surprise, she broke out into peals of laughter, a joyous sound, even to her own ears, and then she winked back at Papu.

'There you go,' she presented her case to the impromptu jury. 'Agni's reputation is hardly that of an unblemished lily. We will appear like fools if we extend unconditional support to him.'

Finally, it was decided that Agni would voluntarily not report for duty for the following five days. He would use this time to introspect and apologize to Seema.

During the ensuing lull in the conversation, Girish took the opportunity to introduce Mishti to Dita, since Palash, who was busy attending to self-perceived slights to his ego, showed no interest in doing the formalities. To Dita's surprise, Mishti did not hold back her appreciation, 'This was truly a sight to see, Palash kaka has met his match at last!' she enthused and leaned in to whisper, 'No wonder Pom has lost his heart to you! It was so worth losing, I must say.'

Dita was puzzled, 'Pom who?' In the anxiety of the last few hours, she found it difficult to focus on a name she had never paid particular attention to.

This was hardly the response Mishti had expected.

It was at this juncture that Aditya Pundit walked into the room, followed by two attendants who were struggling under the weight of an enormous object which appeared to be a life-size portrait of a man, mounted within a heavy wooden frame embellished with vines and roses. Papu and Pinku could not believe their eyes, for in front of them, snug and comfortable in the incongruous setting, was the portrait of their grandfather, Durjoy Pundit, the fabled dacoit of Phulpukur.

'The portrait is ready at last,' Aditya announced with immense pride, looking around for approval. 'It was supposed to go up in the hall of fame, but since we don't have anything like that yet, where do you all suggest that I put this up?'

No one really knew where to put this monstrosity, and

even Girish seemed to have lost his tongue. Finally, Palash croaked, 'Put it up there.' Everyone turned around to look at him: he was pointing to the patch of wall just above Dita's chair, at the head of the elegant rosewood table.

Bob Banerjee, who had wrapped up shooting for the day, had come up to meet Dita in her office. 'Just the appropriate revenge,' he nodded in approval, as everyone gaped at him. 'If the portrait decides to take a tumble while Dita is sitting in that chair, it might just start her off on the highway to heaven.

'I'll make a note of this,' he continued, 'hidden-in-plain-sight murder weapon that will be used to kill the unsuspecting principal in my series. What an innovative idea,' he chuckled.

Tamali, who had followed Bob into the room, blanched at the macabre thought; the blood-red bindi on her forehead seemed iridescent with fury! If looks could kill, Palash Bose would have been dead a couple of times by now, since nearly everyone in the room was giving him nasty looks.

11

Christmas Carol

Christmas was in the air, and Biltu, the office boy, was relieved. For the last few days before the college closed for the winter break, he had been worked off his feet, running around to meet the strident demands of the teachers as well as the office staff. Finally, they had all gone home for the holidays; Biltu cleaned up after them as much as he could, padlocked the main gate of the college, and eagerly walked out into two weeks of freedom. He had plans of going to Kolkata with his two sisters: they wanted to visit the zoo, see the National Museum, take a ride in a phaeton around the Victoria Memorial, and do all the things one does on a winter's day in Kolkata.

Indeed, winter is a craze for the denizens of Kolkata; it's that time of the year when they pull out their monkey caps and oversized cardigans, and women start matching their saris and kurtas with the Kashmiri shawls they have accumulated over the years. It is that time of year when you indulge in nolen-gur sandesh and rasogolla and queue up in front of Flurys to have a slice of their plum cakes, then hop across to Nahoum's in New Market to wallow in the sinful delight of their signature fruit cakes. It's the season of indulgence, after all!

Thus it was on a crisp winter morning that Arko finally

managed to convince Dita that it was worth queuing up for breakfast at Flurys. Arko's enthusiasm was infectious, to say the least, and soon Dita found herself ordering a huge and sumptuous breakfast. 'I'll never be able to finish so much food,' she sighed, but ordered it nonetheless.

For Arko, it was like picking from a wish list. He ordered huevos rancheros, the Spanish-style breakfast served with fried eggs, spicy bacon, and Cajun grilled chicken with a choice of bread and juice on the side. 'That's enough to feed an army for two days,' moaned Dita. Arko had no such worries, and waited eagerly for the food.

The sounds of the clinking cutlery, the whispered conversations, the delicious aromas wafting in the air added up to a feeling of carefree lassitude; it's the nearest to earthly bliss right now, Dita thought as she sipped her tea. Arko, however, was a bundle of energy, and wanted Dita to fill him in on the latest anecdotes from her college.

'Nothing much is happening now, Arko. I want this holiday to be relaxed and peaceful,' Dita said, eyeing the trays of pastries, trying to decide if she had the appetite to indulge in one.

'How about lover boy? Have you seen him lately?' Arko persisted.

'One swallow does not a summer make,' unbidden and unwanted, a wisp of a shadow floated into the day, reflected in the sudden pinched look on Dita's face. 'You cannot call him my lover boy on the strength of two encounters and a phone call. Next thing I know, you'll have a steady girlfriend, and I'll still be trying to figure out what Raja is up to,' Dita teased her brother. 'Finish your food and then we can order some cakes?'

Arko's face lit up at the prospect of finishing off this scrumptious breakfast with cake. He now thought it worthwhile to share some gems of wisdom with his sister. 'Didi, you are not exactly a simpering girl from the nineteenth century, waiting for the man to take the initiative. Get a grip! What's the point of wallowing in self-pity—if you are really interested in him pick up that stupid phone of yours and call him. You should have his number because he called you on the day you got lost.'

Dita pretended to be immersed in the dessert menu while her mind let out a silent whoop of pleasure: she had saved Raja's number, if it was indeed his number that he had called from. She surreptitiously checked her phone, as Arko winked at her across the table, polishing off the last morsels from his plate. 'Go ahead,' he encouraged. 'Don't mind me.'

Crushing the last vestige of indecision, Dita hit the call icon on her screen. The response from the other end was immediate, 'Don't tell me you are lost again?' the voice teased.

'Yes,' Dita's voice shimmered with a smile. 'I had to lose my mind before I called you.'

'Lost or not, it's always a pleasure to hear your voice,' Raja sounded genuinely pleased.

'So what are you up to nowadays?' he slid into the conversation effortlessly. 'I gather it's winter break for you?'

'A much needed one too,' quipped Dita, 'a two-week break from Palash Bose's antics! That fellow is intent on driving me mad,' Dita confided in Raja, thinking he was the only person in Phulpukur who could hold his own against that wily fox. In fact, she had seen him hold fort against

Palash quite a few times.

There was a significant pause before Raja asked the obvious question, 'What has he done now?'

Dita laughed, 'Ask me what he has not done to inconvenience me! It's a long story Raja, too much to narrate over the phone. I'll tell you in person one of these days!'

'Name the day,' Raja, as always, believed in specifics. He was not one to be left dangling.

'Are you in Phulpukur now?' Dita asked.

Again, another short pause, before Raja answered, 'No, not in Phulpukur. I'm in Delhi.'

It's always so difficult to figure out this man's whereabouts. 'What are you doing in Delhi?' she asked.

'You want to ask me all this over the phone, is it?' Raja dodged the question. 'I'm taking the early morning flight to Kolkata tomorrow, in case you still want to meet me? Salt Lake is rather close to the airport, is it not?' Raja prodded, overriding the silent indecision apparent from her side. 'We can grab a quick breakfast somewhere and listen to your tales of woe. I still have the morning at my disposal, after which I have some family matters to attend to.'

'So, you are not quite the lone wolf I imagined, you too have a family?' Dita hedged, wondering if it was wise to give in so easily to Raja's demand.

Raja sighed; family wasn't something he wanted to discuss with Dita right now. 'Let's deal with your Palash Bose induced problems first and talk about my family later?' he sounded cautious and sensible.

A faint trace of uneasiness crept into the conversation: Dita wondered why Raja was so secretive about his family. But she arranged to meet him at the airport, worried that he would disappear if she failed to meet him in the morning. She was annoyed but agreed, nonetheless.

Arko, who had eavesdropped shamelessly on the conversation, had quite a few questions for his sister once it was over. 'What was he doing in Delhi?' he asked. 'What does he generally do besides serving you tea?'

Dita was immediately on the defensive, 'He served me tea only once,' she gave Arko a sheepish glance. 'I have no idea what he actually does; I'm clueless about what he was doing in Delhi too.'

Arko, by now so full of food and cakes that he seemed ready to burst, settled into a state of torpor engaging only a limited part of his brain to figure out Dita's mystery man.

'Who is his brother? Any idea about his family?' Arko sighed with disbelief when he realized Dita knew absolutely nothing.

The only glimmer of hope at the end of a very dark tunnel was that since this man was flying in and out of Delhi, he could not exactly be a pauper. 'Maybe he is an agent for RAW or something, they have their headquarters in Delhi,' he surmised. 'That accounts for all this weird secrecy.' Goggle-eyed, Dita tried to make sense of Arko's theories.

That evening, over dinner, Dita shared Arko's ideas with her mother. Tamali was openly dubious, 'Arko has all sorts of crazy ideas, he might as well convince you that Raja is an intergalactic time traveller,' she huffed.

Arko, however, was convinced that he was right. 'Just you wait, Raja will have a deluge of skeletons popping out of his cupboard,' he predicted.

The next morning, Raja's behaviour at the airport was

distinctly strange. Spotting Dita as he walked out of the arrival gates, he quickly rushed her off to a waiting car. He seemed acutely nervous about something, Dita realized, as she noticed lines of worry carved on that strikingly attractive face. She was at an utter loss as to why Raja appeared to be in such a tearing hurry; out of the corner of her eye she thought she saw three men with cameras running towards them, two women carrying garlands were also trying to catch up. Before she could figure out what was happening, the car managed to execute a smooth exit out of the arrival area. Why does he have a chauffeur-driven car? Arko's assumptions kept popping up at the back of her mind.

Once inside the car, Raja appeared somewhat relieved and his intense grey eyes lit up with pleasure. 'It's been almost three months since I last saw you, hasn't it?' There was such simplicity and innocence in his tone that Dita was almost ready to ignore everything. However, curiosity got the better of her. 'Who were those people chasing you? Why do you have a chauffeur-driven car? Where are we going?' Dita looked at Raja with something akin to suspicion.

Raja pretended to be baffled, 'Who was chasing me?'

'Those people with cameras, I think I saw Chirag Mukherjee, the notorious paparazzo,' Dita tried to look back, but by now the car had gathered so much speed she could not even see the arrival area, let alone the people waiting there.

'Why would people with cameras chase me, Dita? I am hardly Shah Rukh Khan,' Raja laughed out loud. 'As for this car, my brother sent it for me. This is his company's car and it will drop me off at his place.'

He glanced at Dita, trying to figure out whether he had

been convincing enough, and added, 'If you don't mind, I'll just take a few minutes to dump my luggage and then we can go out.'

Dita looked back at him intently. There was such a glaring difference between the unassuming boy that she had first met and this smart and handsome young man, that she remained doubtful. Arko had told her that intelligence agents were masters of disguise and could pull off different kinds of looks convincingly. But that still did not answer the question as to why people were running after him with cameras.

The chessmen in Raja's mind were undoubtedly skittish today. Picking up waves of anxiety from Dita, they were confused over how to play out the next couple of moves. He realized he had already made a few sloppy ones in his eagerness to meet her; he should have anticipated that the press would be sure to follow him today. He had won the Delhi International Chess Championship two days ago, defeating one of the Russian grandmasters, and a couple of journalists in Kolkata, especially Chirag Mukherjee, were quite desperate to get their sound bites.

Considering the fact that Dita was still on a path of headlong collision with Palash Bose, Raja did not want to divulge his identity until he was absolutely sure about her feelings for him. *The moment she finds out that I'm Anuraj Bose she will do a thorough background check and find out I'm Palash Bose's son*, Raja thought glumly. Just the perfect way to sabotage any romantic notion. But he would not give up without a fight, he decided valiantly.

Dita was wearing a modest white Fabindia tunic, paired with turquoise blue Ria Menorca espadrilles, and Raja found it extremely difficult to tear his eyes away from this dainty vision. 'Stop staring,' Dita scolded as they stepped out of the car and took the lift up to Pom's apartment.

Holding the door for Dita to enter, Raja wheeled his luggage into Pom's apartment. Situated on the thirtieth floor, it had a picturesque view of the city. The furniture was sparse yet reflected quiet elegance. Raja must have a gem of a brother, Dita thought, as her eyes fell on an assortment of fruits and cereals set out on the dining table, alongside two pitchers of cold milk and iced lemon tea, and a small bowl of honey.

Raja sent out a mental hug to Pom, who had obviously tried his best to provide breakfast for Raja before he left for the office. 'Perfect opportunity for me to play host,' Raja joked, breezily asking Dita to help herself to the food and tea.

Dita smiled nostalgically. 'Hardly the kind of tea that you served me on my first day of college; this looks so plush, that was so earthy,' quite unconsciously, she leaned in towards him, caught in that sweet little moment from the past. When she looked up, and she really had to look a long way up, she found those bewitching grey eyes boring down into her soul. What happens if I want to kiss him now? she wondered irreverently, I won't even be able to reach up to him; she was reminded of a Karan Johar movie in which Jaya had to stand on a footstool just to hug Amitabh. This mental image convinced her of the absurdity of her desire to kiss Raja, and she turned away.

Raja was puzzled by the mixed signals Dita was sending out. One moment the chessmen in his mind were dancing with glee at her come-hither looks, and the next they fell flat on their face as her mood changed dramatically. So he made what he thought was a smart move—beating a hasty retreat to refresh himself before venturing out to explore the city.

Dita heaved a sigh of relief as Raja disappeared. She felt very unsure of herself and had a lurking suspicion that Raja was hiding something from her. At the same time her subconscious mind seemed to urge her on to seize the day, regardless of the consequences.

High time I stopped overthinking the situation, Dita scolded herself as she poured herself a tall glass of iced lemon tea, added a teaspoonful of honey, and sipped it while looking down at the city. Somewhere behind the walls, she could hear strains of Billy Joel belting out 'The Stranger' and Raja was whistling along with the music. Quite significant, she noted absent-mindedly.

The fog blanketing the early morning Kolkata cityscape was dissipating gradually, although a few strands lingered on to play peekaboo with the hazy sunlight. Perched atop her eyrie, she could imagine the wind rustling through the greenery as the city got ready for another hectic day. A silence engulfed her, a peace so deep that it seemed to immerse her in its endless depth and she felt as light as a feather floating atop the city.

And then the world tilted on its axis. Two strong arms were lifting her up, those grey eyes twinkling with mischief, headful of damp hair still glistening with moisture, and she melted into the embrace. Droplets of water splashed onto her cheeks as Raja playfully shook out his hair; her laughter was a joyous sound as she raised her face in a silent invitation.

Raja stared at her for an endless moment, before

swooping down to claim her lips with a feverish passion. Days of anxiety and indecision burnt out in the blazing heat of the embrace, yet the fear of rejection kept eroding Raja's confidence as he tried to brush aside the dark secrets of his identity. Who knows how this lady, snug as a kitten in his embrace, will react once she finds out his true identity? Will he really have to pay for the sins of his father?

Pushing the dismal thoughts aside ruthlessly, he waded deep into the kiss; she tasted of honey and lemon, he thought, as he nibbled her lips, and plundered the sweetest mouth. Pom is again here by proxy, he noted, it's his iced lemon tea that is the flavour of this embrace.

Dita trembled under the sensuous onslaught. The silver bangles she had borrowed from Tamali clinked crazily against the glass in her hands. Tea and Raja together spelled mischief: caught up in their embrace, the glass nearly slipped from Dita's hands, spilling tea onto her kurta. Cold rivulets from the tall glass ran across her skin, seeping through her flimsy tunic, rendering it semi-transparent. The honey in the tea wreaked further havoc. 'You are one sticky mess,' Raja whispered as he nuzzled into the warmth of her skin.

The ice from the drink and the heat of her skin were doing strange things to Raja's equilibrium as he settled her down on the sofa. She pulled him in with her, refusing to let him go. Carried away by the intoxicating scent of the honey, he hungrily kissed her lips, her face, and neck. His hands seemed to have a mind of their own as they explored her petite form, a curious bundle of softness and feral heat which was determined to set him aflame. 'Pom will kill me,' he was stricken with sudden remorse. 'We are messing up his sofa.'

'Let's change positions, then. You are less sticky than

me,' she said, pushing him back on the sofa, pulling back a little to enjoy the view. Startled grey eyes looked back at her as she gently nudged two sticky fingers into his mouth. His head fell back as his tongue rolled around the honeyed intruders. 'Let's make this the best honey lemon tea you ever had, Raja,' she whispered, nibbling his ears till he was left gasping for breath. Feeling the wetness of her tunic against his skin, his hands implored her to take it off; she raised her head again, regal as a swan, as she drank in the sight of her beautiful boy.

Dita eased herself out of the embrace, stood up, took off her tunic with languid ease, and unclasped her bra; she bent down and pulled up the dazed boy, 'We've made a mess of this sofa, let's find a bed to mess around on properly.'

Raja's voice sounded hoarse even to his own ears, 'Are you sure, Dita?'

'Yes,' she whispered, as she melted into him, skin on fire with desire. 'Never more so!'

Raja picked her up with a whoop, heading towards the bedroom, when she murmured, 'Who is Pom?'

Raja was surprised at the query; he looked down at her with frank curiosity, 'Why?'

'Mishti told me someone called Pom is in love with me,' she muttered as she covered Raja's gasp of surprise with a hot and demanding kiss.

12

The Remains of the Day

The two brothers gave up the idea of driving back to Phulpukur that evening, heading out to Park Street for dinner instead. The air around them buzzed with awareness of the merriment to come with Christmas. Shop fronts twinkled with fairy lights and Christmas trees in full-blown decor vied for the attention of the pedestrians. Peter Cat, as usual, had a small queue of expectant diners up front; Pom and Raja waited patiently for their table.

Pom leaned back on one of the pillars in front of the restaurant and lit a cigarette. His eyes followed the ring of smoke as he said, 'Ma would have expected us back home today.'

'I know,' Raja looked away from Pom. 'I needed to clear my head before I go back to Phulpukur. Baba's behaviour in matters of the college has been far from exemplary.'

Pom blew out another ring of smoke and waited for further explanation from Raja.

Raja reached out for the cigarette from Pom's hand and tried blowing a smoke ring himself, 'Now we both look like Gandalf, when he comes back to the Shire in *The Lord of the Rings*.' Raja looked at his brother affectionately, 'Thank you for that lovely breakfast too,' he smiled. 'The only meal I had today.'

Pom remained silent; he had always been akin to a father confessor to Raja and knew his brother had had a tumultuous day and just wanted to talk and unwind.

Raja eyed Pom speculatively, 'You know somehow I always feel your presence between Dita and me. You may not believe this but today, bang in the middle of everything else, she asked me, "Who is Pom?"'

'That's way below the belt, you mean to tell me that she does not remember me at all?' Pom boxed Raja's ears in mock anger. 'For fuck's sake, the girl is decimating my ego,' he laughed. 'And here I thought I had made a significant impact when I met her.'

'Zilch, nada, nothing whatsoever!' Raja merrily added salt to Pom's wound. A shattered look descended on Pom's face. Raja was puzzled, had he somehow managed to hurt Pom's feelings? Surely not?

But Pom was not even looking at Raja, his gaze was fixed on something behind his shoulders. Raja followed his gaze; a girl had stepped out of a massive SUV and was approaching them with grim determination.

'Oh fuck,' were the only words that popped out of Raja's mouth. The relaxed atmosphere disappeared just as rapidly as the smoke rings had vanished into thin air as Mishti frogmarched the two brothers into the restaurant. 'My father's name is enough to secure a table almost everywhere in this city,' Mishti offered by way of explanation as a liveried waiter indicated their table.

'I guess all of us will want to have the chelo kebabs,' she informed the waiter, then turned towards the brothers, 'you can order your drinks, perhaps?'

'Screwdriver,' the brothers intoned dully, since it was

apparent that they were about to be royally screwed by Mishti.

Mishti's appearance today was far removed from her usual salwar-clad self. Dressed in form-fitting black jeans and an animal print silk shirt, her hair tied back with an intricate clasp, she resembled a deadly feline on the prowl.

'How did you know where to find us?' Raja was perplexed.

'Being my father's daughter sometimes has its upside too,' Mishti owned up demurely. 'I had Pom followed.'

Raja choked on his screwdriver, Pom spluttered, but Mishti seemed unperturbed, content and confident.

'My men have been following Pom for the last few weeks,' she went on with an air of unconcern, 'ever since I found out that Dita does not even know who he is! So, I ask myself, here is a girl who has no freaking clue who Pom is, and Pom is telling me that he will marry her?' She gave Pom a cold hard glare, 'Perhaps you would like to explain?'

Raja wondered how Pom was going to extricate himself from this grave of his own digging. Would he be able to tell Mishti outright that he wasn't looking forward to mafioso links in his life? Would he be able to tell her that and walk away from this place alive?

The chelo kebabs arrived: succulent morsels of chicken and mutton seekh kebabs on a bed of fragrant rice, topped with dollops of golden butter and fried egg. It was too good to be kept waiting and Raja and Pom gave it their wholehearted attention, ignoring Mishti's query.

Seeing that the brothers did not seem keen on offering explanations, Mishti tried another tack. 'I completely understand why you are so bowled over by this girl, Pom, though I don't see when and how you met her? She is absolutely worthy of being your dream girl; I have never seen anyone stand up so boldly for what she thought was right against a room full of old foxes!' She stopped to gauge the impact her words were having.

Two pairs of brilliant grey eyes were trained on her now. In a voice reflecting quiet admiration, Mishti continued, 'It was a sight to see, that waif of a girl did not give an inch, she just took her due.'

Raja gave Pom a significant glance, this must be the backstory of Dita's recent animosity with their father. Pom sniggered; Raja, for obvious reasons, had not been able to discuss those issues with Dita. Conversely, Dita was still in the dark about Raja.

'I learned a lesson that day,' Mishti nodded emphatically. 'It's worth putting up a fight for what you want.'

Raja, yet again, found his heart filling with admiration for Mishti; she might try to act sophisticated, but she was just a young girl at heart. Raja leaned forward and took her hand in his. 'It's totally worth fighting for,' he reassured her.

Pom's eyebrows hit the ceiling, 'What will you be fighting for?' He had a sinking sensation that he already knew the answer.

'For you, Pom, only for you,' Mishti sounded thoroughly convinced.

'You go, girl,' Raja said enthusiastically. 'Now that we are sorted, let's order some dessert,' he ignored Pom's furious glare and signalled the waiter for the menu.

'Do you need any more drinks to fortify yourself, Mishti?' Raja asked with mock concern. 'The way I see it, Pom will not go out without a fight either.'

'And the way I see it,' Pom reminded Raja, 'Baba was trying to fix you up with Mishti; by the time we reach Phulpukur, he might already have a date in mind to marry you two off,' he finished smugly.

Raja's face fell like a punctured balloon, 'Sins of the father,' he intoned.

Mishti, however, was in no mood to be beaten down. 'Let us call the shots, this time around,' she was emphatic.

Raja appeared baffled. 'And just how do we do that? Your father and mine call all the shots in Phulpukur and Diamond Harbour.'

All this while Pom had been studying Mishti's reactions, trying to ascertain the gravity of her thoughts. 'I guess she is talking about subverting the power structure,' he mused. 'Guerrilla tactics, maybe?'

Mishti gave a nod of confirmation before explaining how she proposed to handle the situation. 'Some of my father's men are loyal to me. If push comes to shove I'll ask them to kidnap Raja and hold him in some undisclosed location till we ride out the storm.'

Hell's bells, thought Raja. The nightmare persists.

Meanwhile, Pom was having a good laugh at Raja's expense, 'Fantastic! If you can really pull this off, you will be depriving two wily old men of the greatest pleasure of their lives!'

13

Hard Times

*I*t was with a heavy heart that Biltu unlocked the gates of the college; now that the holidays were over, he was positively anxious about the forthcoming session. The college grapevine had it on good authority that changes were afoot and many a battle would be won or lost over the principal's rosewood table. The students' council election was around the corner, and everyone in the village awaited it with much trepidation.

Palash Bose knew that his mandate would be to ensure smooth success for Shyamol Sathi. Dita had no inkling of the political drama that was about to unfold. In her last posting as a part-time lecturer in a Kolkata girls' college, no one was really interested in politicking and she had seen girls literally forcing others to contest the seats. She had no idea how out of depth she would be in the impending elections in Phulpukur College.

Incidentally, this was the first time that the students of Phulpukur College would be contesting for the council; they had not been able to do so hitherto because the college did not have a campus of its own, which is a prerequisite to hold the elections. Now that the campus was ready, Raktokarobi and Shyamol Sathi were ready to fight it out to the bitter end. Banners and party manifestos were printed and ready to be pasted on freshly painted walls. The Raktokarobi party symbol, sporting the five-petalled, funnel-shaped red oleanders offset by green foliage of lance-shaped leaves, vied for pride of place with the Shyamol Sathi logo of the verdant clover plant set against a stark white backdrop, its four leaves ostensibly representing faith, hope, love, and luck.

Dita was confounded by the very notion of candidates putting up their posters on any available space in the college. 'Absolutely not! I cannot allow them to deface the walls of the college with their ugly posters. Candidates who are contesting can go and make their pitch to students in individual classes. That should be more than enough.'

Alok, who knew the ground reality of such elections, chose to disagree. 'They do not listen to reason once they are incited in the name of politics. The boundaries of respect between a teacher and student are hopelessly eroded in the heat of the moment.'

Sahana was perturbed too. 'They behave like fanatics. I've seen them in action, it's quite dangerous,' she warned Dita. 'Be very careful about the decisions you make.'

Dita instructed Alok to issue a notice asking the students to refrain from putting up posters on the walls. She then turned her attention to more pressing and worthwhile matters: the college had applied for several new subjects in the undergraduate pass course, English being one of them.

The challenge was that when the subject-matter experts from Calcutta University came to ascertain whether the college had adequate resources to support the course, it was essential to have a good stock of books on the various subjects in the library. Unfortunately, that was the most obvious pitfall for her college: there was no library and there were no books. Trying to circumvent this problem, Dita had brought in a significant chunk of her own collection of literary texts. This morning she was busy erasing her name from most of them; she would donate them to the college, she thought.

⌣

Dita looked out of her window and saw Bob Banerjee and his team of actors trooping in with their crew. Three of the most popular stars from Bob's production house would be shooting their scenes today, Tamali had informed her. Pushing the books away Dita went out to join her mother while the shots were being arranged.

Tamali pointed out to Dita the three charismatic actors who raked in popular viewership for Bob's web series. While Dita was admiring them from afar, Tamali was surprised to find Biltu placing a red plastic chair next to her. An elegant woman approached them. She was dressed in a simple red and white cotton sari, her hair was tied back with a string of fresh jasmines, framing a face of unusual beauty; Tamali noticed that she walked with a slight limp.

When Hemlata smiled, the smile lit up her eyes. She had not been able to control her excitement when she heard that Rahul Sen, Prithvi Thakur, and Dhruv Mukherjee were all set to shoot today and as a diehard fan, she could not let this opportunity slip. She had also recognized Tamali, her signature red bindi adding a piquant warmth to her face as she waited on the sidelines.

'Namoshkar, I'm Hemlata,' she introduced herself to Tamali. Her Bengali was not perfect, but delivered in a lilting tone, it was pleasant. 'You must be Tamali Roy. I've seen you in so many roles that your face is the most familiar one in this crowd. It's such a pleasure to meet you in person.'

Hemlata's smile was so sincere, so genuine, that Tamali immediately felt herself warming to this winsome woman. 'I feel so glad when people actually tell me that they remember me even from my minor roles,' Tamali confessed to Hemlata, instinctively reaching out to take her hands, her tinkling bangles sounding a merry note of approval. 'It makes me feel good about myself, you know?'

Hemlata sat down on the plastic chair, sometimes her legs hurt if she stood for too long. 'I really like your work, Tamali, your shows have often been like a lifeline to me,' she looked down at her legs, hidden under the folds of her sari. 'Since I cannot run around that much, I'm mostly at home, reading my books or watching some web series or the other.'

Hemlata's gaze shifted to Dita and another dazzling smile followed. Something shifted in Dita's subconscious mind, an unacknowledged recognition, a fleeting feeling of familiarity, as she watched the graceful grey-eyed woman. 'You must be Dita, I have heard so much about you,' Hemlata said gently. 'In fact I keep hearing about you, day in and day out.'

Dita was puzzled, why would Hemlata keep hearing about her, was she that popular in Phulpukur? Or unpopular?

Oblivious to Dita's unease, Hemlata continued, 'I would like to donate some books too, if it helps in your efforts? I have quite a lot on philosophy and history.'

Dita was curious, 'Forgive me if I'm missing something, but how did you know that we are applying for history and philosophy honours?'

'Oh dear, it's so remiss of me,' Hemlata apologized. 'I

know a lot about this college because my husband is the president of the governing body.'

Dita gasped. This beautiful woman was married to that old fox! Some of the enthusiasm that she had experienced upon meeting Hemlata dissipated at the mention of Palash Bose. But if the lady wanted to help, who was she to deny her? Dita excused herself politely on the pretext of having a class to teach and moved away.

Hemlata smiled ruefully at Tamali, 'No love lost between those two, and I know just how difficult Palash can be at times.'

Tamali smiled, 'Oh! My daughter is a stubborn one too! Leave those two to their devices and concentrate on those three handsome men over there. Would you like to meet them?'

'Definitely,' Hemlata said. She fished for her phone in her bag, 'Let me call Mishti, she would love to meet you all! You have a diehard fan there!'

Tamali nodded, 'I think I met her once; very enthusiastic girl.'

The three young men came over happily on being beckoned by Tamali; Bob was busy haranguing his camera crew so the three actors were at a loose end. Hemlata waved to Biltu to fetch some more chairs. 'This is quite a smart campus for a village. I did not really expect such a sprawling one,' observed Dhruv. 'Bob is so happy with the location, he cannot make up his mind in which of his favourite spots he wants to start shooting today.'

Prithvi, meanwhile, was gazing with rapt attention at Hemlata. 'Why appreciate the campus only when I am in the presence of such beautiful people?'

Tamali laughed, as Hemlata blushed, 'Always the flirt, Prithvi!'

Rahul settled down beside Hemlata. 'But why can't he say that she is beautiful, when she is so obviously breathtaking? Beauty lies in the eye of the beholder, does it not?' he added, giving Hemlata a frank look.

Hemlata could not remember the last time Palash had looked at her with appreciation in his eyes or commented on her beauty; he was a thoroughly practical man and she was just a fixture in the daily routine of his life and a mother to his children. A long time ago, she had reconciled herself to her fate and had not complained even once. This afternoon, however, it felt nice to be the centre of attention, however contrived or false it may be, to feel happy for a fleeting moment and not have a care in the world beyond this circle of joy.

Bob joined the group, having settled the last details for the shoot. Looking with unabashed enthusiasm at Hemlata, he asked, 'Who is this charming lady to whom I have not been introduced?'

'So dramatic, all of you,' Hemlata chuckled. 'But you've made me feel so good, flirting for the first time at this ripe old age seems to work wonders. I'm so glad I met you all today! I have been an avid fan for so long, now I finally get to know you behind the silver screen; you are so much more fun than I expected! And no starry tantrums?'

'No such luck for us,' Rahul pulled off a dramatic moue of disappointment. 'The lion's share of tantrums in this crew goes to Bob! We are all left pandering to his ego so much that we do not have time for ourselves.'

'You ingrate!' Bob chased Rahul, roaring with mock

pique. The group dispersed on a wave of good humour; the shot was ready, and the camera was ready to roll.

Hemlata held Tamali back for a few seconds, 'Would it be too much of an imposition to ask you for autographs from all of you? I would love to have them as a memento from this afternoon and share them with Anupam and Anuraj.'

Tamali was touched: while fans regularly asked for autographs from the popular actors and Bob, very rarely did they approach her; Hemlata asking for her autograph too seemed to be such a thoughtful gesture.

'Of course,' Tamali said happily. 'I'll see to it,' and then out of curiosity she asked, 'Who are they, Anupam and Anuraj? Do you want Prithvi, Rahul, and Dhruv to write any specific messages for them?'

'It's for my sons,' Hemlata replied. 'They'll just be happy to see that I have secured autographs from actors I keep gushing over. My sons keep me company at times, but they are not avid watchers.'

During the next two hours of shooting, the names of Hemlata's sons kept floating around in Tamali's consciousness. She kept wondering what exactly she was trying to figure out; the vermilion of her bindi started throbbing like the proverbial third eye, and she was sure she was missing something.

Anupam and Anuraj.

Hemlata was married to Palash Bose.

Anupam Bose and Anuraj Bose.

She had heard the name Anuraj Bose mentioned somewhere. But where?

She looked up, one of the cameras was focused on her face. A few feet away Bob was poring over a monitor screen.

Shadows shifted and scattered; and then the pieces of the puzzle slowly fell into place. Of course! She had seen that name on the television screen; several anchors and newsreaders had mentioned that name.

Anuraj Bose. The chess prodigy.

He was Hemlata's son?

14

Bleak House

*U*tpal could not believe his eyes. The principal had actually put up a notice restricting election posters inside the campus; in Utpal's mind it seemed tantamount to infringement of one's constitutional rights. Unsure of how to react, he fished out his phone from his pocket and dialled Arshad Ali's number.

Arshad was one of the representatives of Raktokarobi's high command; patience had never been his forte and thus, when Utpal called him to sort out the issue regarding campaign posters, his trigger-happy instincts went into overdrive.

'How can you let this woman call the shots?' Belligerence boiled over in his tone. 'She has no clue as to how student elections are conducted.'

'Dita ma'am is generally very neutral and level-headed,' Utpal reasoned with Arshad. 'She really helped us out in Seema's case, if you remember?'

Arshad remained unconvinced. 'Shyamol Sathi has a stronger presence than us, they will not abide by the principal's petty restrictions. We have to act before they come in forcibly and put up their posters all over the college walls.

'This woman is the root of all problems here,' Arshad's rant continued. 'We cannot allow her to interfere in all matters. Pick her up when she drives out of Phulpukur today. Let me drill some sense into her!'

'Pick her up?' Utpal repeated stupidly; his agitated fingers found a small hole in the sleeve of his frayed red T-shirt and started to pull at it in silent disquiet.

'Yes, yes,' Arshad cut in impatiently. 'I'll send some of my men to your college with a car. You take charge from there and bring her over to our party office in Maniktala. I'll wait for you there.'

'But, Arshad, that's like kidnapping,' squealed Utpal; the hole in the sleeve gaped open as his alarmed fingers unconsciously dug deeper into the frayed fabric.

'Keep your voice down,' came the irritated reply. 'It's hardly a kidnapping; we will just let her understand the error of her ways and let her go. No need for you to lose sleep over this!'

Utpal was in a quandary—Arshad was a man of limited intellectual resources and unlimited unsavoury skills. Although duty-bound to follow Arshad's dictates, Utpal wasn't convinced about the viability of such a fishy scheme.

Unbeknownst to Utpal, matters were to be taken out of his hand, for standing a few feet away, pretending to study the noticeboard and impatiently pushing back his greasy hair was Rajeev, the self-appointed student leader of Shyamol Sathi. He had eavesdropped unashamedly and inched closer to Utpal, who was in a tizzy and literally shouting into the phone, hence it was not very difficult to figure out what Arshad and he were up to.

As soon as Utpal disappeared on the lawns beyond the office, flailing his arms in desperation, Rajeev dashed into an empty classroom, dialled Palash's number and swiftly repeated what he had overheard.

Palash was nonplussed. 'Pick her up? She is hardly a sack of potatoes that they are going to pick up anytime they want to! Besides, she is a very difficult woman. If she has decided not to comply she will put up a fight,' Palash added, as he paced up and down the length of his small library. 'We cannot let Raktokarobi intimidate us like this, we will have to counter their move, stop their hare-brained schemes.

'Gherao seems to be the only solution,' Palash continued in a contemplative tone, as if he was weighing the pros and cons of the situation. 'Do you have enough students to stage a gherao, Rajeev? You'll have to act fast and take everyone by surprise; no one must be allowed to leave the college campus.'

Rajeev supported the idea enthusiastically. 'My boys will be ready to act at a moment's notice, sir, and I'll ask them to be discreet.'

'It will be easy to arrange the gherao and set up your picketing lines on the campus,' Palash mused. 'Fortunately, the college has only one point of entry or exit so you will just need to lock the main gate of the campus. Ask your boys to prepare themselves to hold the gate for a couple of hours at the very least. Do it as soon as possible. This will totally sabotage Arshad's plans and if Dita gives in to the demands of your party, Shyamol Sathi will be the uncontested winner in the forthcoming elections.'

'Brilliant plan, sir,' Rajeev was raring to go. 'What demands should we place?'

'Ask the college authority to allow you to put up your manifestos; ask them to give you adequate time during college hours to speak to the students and counsel them in your favour,' Palash advised. 'I am sure Dita will not comply, at least initially, so be ready for a long drawn-out gherao. Make sure you have enough food and water, you might be called upon to provide essentials inside too.' Palash reiterated the ground rules, 'You will not let violence intrude at any point of time. And keep me posted.'

Head buzzing with instructions to be executed immediately, Rajeev ran to gather his troops around him. Meanwhile, Palash, who had sounded very confident during the conversation, was hyperventilating internally; he prayed that things would go smoothly and it would not be a problematic protest. But unfortunately, he had not taken into consideration the unreliability of his own temper.

As it turned out, both fate and family were at odds with him.

Just as Rajeev had eavesdropped on Utpal's conversation, so also had Raja been a silent audience to his father's conversation while Palash was busy formulating his plans with the Shyamol Sathi student leader. Raja had gone to Palash's library looking for a copy of Bobby Fischer's *My 60 Memorable Games*. The library was at a secluded corner of the house where the other members of the household rarely ventured. Raja was shocked and alarmed at the way in which his father was trying to micromanage a gherao.

'You are absolutely incorrigible, you know that, right? You just advised a young boy to organize a gherao?' Raja could hardly conceal the condemnation in his voice.

'Since you heard so much of the conversation, you must have realized that this was the only way we could have stopped Raktokarobi from picking up Dita Roy and making her agree to God knows what? That Arshad fellow is not to be trusted at all.'

'No,' Raja was firm. 'This was not the only way out. You could have called Dita and warned her instead of turning it into a political project to garner cheap publicity for Shyamol Sathi. If Arshad is not to be trusted, Palash Bose, the politician, cannot be trusted too,' Raja's face scrunched up with evident disapproval. 'I think you should call Rajeev and stop it before things get out of hand. Student politics is volatile at best, you never know where it all may end!'

Palash looked at Raja with ill-controlled irritation. 'Plans are already in motion, they cannot be stopped now. I have no intention of retracting them. Sabotaging my plans is what comes to you naturally, for reasons I have never been able to fathom; never have you ever come up with alternatives or more viable solutions. Keep your disapproval to yourself, I have neither the time nor the inclination to listen to your harangue.'

Raja was stung by the evident animosity. 'What alternatives could I have given you? What are you talking about?'

Palash was already striding out of the library, but Raja's query made him stop in his tracks. He turned around and lashed out, 'You are aware, are you not, that if I am to contest for the MLA seat I would need some strong political backing? Right now, I cannot sit back and let Raktokarobi dictate terms for the student elections; it is a political manoeuvre and must be answered on a political platform and that is what I am trying to do! I need to win this round because between you and Pom, you have sabotaged my chances of an alliance with Girish Sarkar. If I had that support, I wouldn't have to look around for smaller factions to prop me up! Girish would have been a huge help.'

Rigid with anger, Palash heaped further recriminations on Raja. 'You are just a selfish brat, busy with your own career in chess. You could have considered Mishti as a good match for yourself too, since Pom was obviously not interested; but no, why would you even want to help your father?'

Raja was taken aback by this visceral attack, 'But marrying Mishti was never an option for me,' he mumbled. 'I already liked someone else.'

At the mention of this apparently unknown someone else, Palash felt the world around him go up in flames of rage; unable to control his fury any longer, he rushed out of the room, closed the door with a resounding bang and locked it. 'All your options are in my hands now,' he roared, shaking his fists in the air. 'Let me see how this someone else helps you.'

As Raja heard Palash's footsteps receding further and further down the corridors, he realized with horror that his father had locked him in a room that very few people visited, and he did not even have a phone to call Pom for help.

15

Kidnapped

Mishti jumped out of the car, almost tripping over in her haste to reach the shooting site. But wait, what were those colourful banners fluttering in the wind, a sea of black heads milling against each other in front of the college gate? Slogans extolling freedom of expression wafted cacophonously into the lazy afternoon air, stirring all those within hearing distance out of their usual siesta-like apathy. Incomprehension clouded her vision. What was happening?

Suddenly, two pairs of strong arms were dragging her backwards and placing a blindfold over her eyes; someone shoved a piece of cloth into her mouth before she could even shriek in alarm. She was picked up unceremoniously and dumped into a waiting vehicle. The engine roared into action.

'Call Arshad and tell him we have the girl,' the rough hands pinning her down had an equally rough voice. 'We did not get Utpal though, I think he got locked inside.'

Arshad was on the speaker, shouting, 'Why would anyone want to lock Utpal in? What the fuck is happening?'

Another voice broke in, trying to explain the situation, 'There is a gherao happening in the college now. Shyamol Sathi supporters have locked the gates and are protesting against something. Many students and teachers are locked inside, I think Utpal too. He was caught by surprise it seems, he did not manage to get out.'

There was a short pause as Arshad processed this information. 'Did anyone see you picking up Dita Roy? You just said there was quite a crowd in front of the main gate, did anyone see you guys grabbing this woman?'

'Absolutely not,' the rough voice was brusque. 'All eyes were on the college gate, no one was interested in what was happening on the opposite side of the road. We are well on our way now...should be reaching Maniktala in an hour or so.'

Arshad appeared to be satisfied and the conversation ended.

Mishti's mind was echoing with silent screams. 'Let me go, let me go, you fucking idiots, I am not Dita Roy!' She jostled around on the car seat, trying to make her fury evident. Being completely ignored by her captors, she continued her vindictive and retributive but muffled rant. 'Just you wait, just you wait, you oafs! Not only have you picked up the wrong girl, you have picked up a dangerous daughter! Once my father finds out about this he is going to make mincemeat out of you.'

But then, she thought forlornly, who is going to inform my father?

♪

Jai was in a bit of a rush, having quite a few errands to run for Girish. After dropping Mishti near the college, he reversed the car and then promptly got stuck amidst a crowd of students rushing towards the college gate. Lowering the window, he peered out trying to figure out what was happening. Young boys and girls were flooding in by the droves with Shyamol Sathi banners, white flags with intertwined lime green clover leaves, their faces shining with excitement as they joined the rhythmic chants that rent the air. As they gathered in a cluster around the college gate, the road ahead of him started to clear up, and through the staggered gaps Jai thought he saw something very strange. Just across the road two men were forcing a girl into a car; judging by her clothes, the girl appeared to be Mishti.

Panic gripped Jai as he tried to make his way through the crowd, horn blaring. The mob in front of him started giving him dirty looks, refusing to move and ignoring the urgent blasts of the horn; Jai watched with disbelief as his car was rapidly engulfed in a human wave. Unsure of what to do he turned off the engine, picked up his phone, dialled Mishti's number, and waited anxiously. Perhaps he was wrong after all, it may not have been Mishti whom he saw being bundled into a black Toyota Innova. The phone was ringing at the other end...it kept ringing but there was no answer. On full throttle panic alert now, Jai dialled Girish's number.

Try as she might to concentrate on the filming of *Now and Again*, a sense of unease gripped Hemlata. Out of the corner of her eye she noticed some commotion around the main gate of the campus. Before her mind could even begin to process what was going on, the iron gates closed shut with a resounding clang and rowdy shouts echoed in the still afternoon air. Hemlata literally jumped out of her skin as frenzied cries shattered the silence that had settled on the campus, 'Dita Roy, hai hai! Hai hai, Dita Roy! Inquilab Zindabad!' Fanatical voices added fuel to fury, blindly demanding and unreasonable, 'Down with shameless oppression! Freedom of expression for all, it's our constitutional right.'

Bob and his crew seemed to be a unit turned to stone; shooting jolted to a stop without any explicit order from anyone; everyone turned towards the commotion with disbelief. By now quite a sizeable crowd had gathered around the gate, banners with lime green leaves unfurled their belligerence and reared their heads beyond the iron gates. It was apparent to everyone inside the campus that they had been locked in, and it could be a long wait before differences were resolved and they could go back home.

Everyone who knew Dita, knew without a doubt that she would not give in to the demands of Shyamol Sathi so easily and would fight it out to the bitter end; until then, everyone would be in suspended animation.

Trying to figure out the reason behind the huge turnout of Shyamol Sathi supporters, Hemlata had a nagging suspicion that it could not have been planned and executed by mere student leaders; this gherao had the hallmarks of a mastermind, and she was in no two minds about his identity.

Palash Bose answered the phone on its second ring, and all hell broke loose. The normally gentle and tolerant Hemlata was beside herself with fury. 'Do you even know what you have done? You have obviously ordered this gherao in Phulpukur College. Don't deny it, I won't believe you! And along with many other unsuspecting people on the campus, you have locked me in too.'

Palash was perplexed. He had noted Hemlata's absence

that morning, but since she had mentioned that she would be visiting Radha, he had concluded that was where she had gone. He had been way too busy in the morning to give the matter much thought. 'What exactly are you doing at the college, Hemlata? And was I supposed to know that you would be there?'

'Since when did you show any interest in what I do?' Hemlata countered. 'You are busy in your own Machiavellian world. Something as trivial as coming to see the shooting of a web series would not capture your imagination, would it?'

Dear lord, thought Palash, that is what the old girl is up to nowadays, running down to the college campus to catch Bob and his crew shooting; but now it is going to be a no-win situation for me, he groaned, Hemlata will want me to call off the gherao, which I obviously won't be able to do, at least not at this juncture.

He was dead right. 'You better do something about this right away, Palash. Surely you don't expect me to wait it out till the students lift the gherao?'

'And what exactly am I supposed to do?'

'Call off your goons. There's a large crowd of people out there, and I'm sure not all of them are students, there must be Shyamol Sathi party workers too. Call them back before things get out of hand.'

'Things are already out of hand,' Palash sounded contemplative. 'Bob's presence on the campus means that this gherao will grab a lot of unrequired attention. That fool of a boy Rajeev failed to tell me this! And Hemlata, whatever you may think, I am not the be-all and end-all of everything, there are many things which are totally out of my control.'

'You are just a miserable man who loves to inflict trouble on people and then you merrily wash your hands of the entire situation,' Hemlata fumed. 'I had invited Mishti to join me at the filming site, but the poor girl must be stranded somewhere in that stupid gherao now and she's not even answering her phone. All this is your fault.'

While Hemlata was busy heaping recriminations on Palash, unbeknownst to them, events of unimaginable magnitude were playing themselves out and adding to the quandary that they were already in.

⌣

The office staff gravitated towards the principal's office with downcast and somewhat furtive expressions on their faces. Nearly all of them were covert Shyamol Sathi supporters, so they did not have much to say apart from voicing discomfort at the prospect of being held back in the college for an unspecified period. The teachers were more vocal in their discontent: Dita could hear Sahana yelling at Pinku over the phone, asking him to step up and stop the gherao.

'Shouting at him will not mend matters now,' Dita tried to pacify Sahana. 'The crowd that has gathered by our main gate will not be dispersed so easily, they have a mandate to follow, I guess.'

The teachers had a suggestion, 'Why don't we call the police to disperse the crowd?'

'Right now, even that might not be a good idea,' Alok offered hesitantly. 'If the police come in and try to forcibly disband the students, some of them might put up active resistance and get hurt in doing so. Such an incident will definitely go against the college authority, who would be seen as colluding with the police to harass the youngsters.'

'Alok is right,' Sahana agreed. 'And if any student is hurt, they will make a martyr out of him or her and keep calling for justice. It's better to wait it out and let them come to a reasonable resolution.'

Dita nodded absent-mindedly. 'So we will wait it out. But the students—how many of them are caught on the campus with us?' She had other thoughts troubling her too: Tamali and Bob's entire crew were also under lockdown, Arko would be all alone this evening. Hardly a comforting thought. Even Raja was not answering her calls, she wondered what was amiss.

'Most of the students had already left to join the Shyamol Sathi cohort out there, it seems,' Dipten observed. 'The ones left inside are a few hapless Raktokarobi supporters and another handful of apolitical kids who couldn't care less if Shyamol Sathi and Raktokarobi fought it out to the death.'

'Round them up and bring them to my office,' Dita instructed. 'I have to reassure them that they are safe with us here.'

While Dipten went out to summon the students, Alok headed out to the college canteen to see whether they could provide some snacks and beverages to fortify them for the long wait ahead. Bob and his team had already packed up. 'Who cares about onscreen drama when you have so much happening in real life?' Bob chortled, as he shared pakoras and tea with his actors and technicians.

Dhruv rifled through the canteen's stores to figure out whether it had sufficient supplies for the unexpected crowd who were now prisoners on the campus.

'If they have dal and chawal we can make khichri and

be sorted for the night too,' joked Prithvi as Rahul, one of the most bankable stars in Bob's stellar cast, and Tamali looked on with glum expressions.

'Dita is a hard nut to crack,' Tamali said morosely. 'You might as well start planning for morning, noon, and night, and God knows how many of them.'

A student who was having tea at the next table started to choke on his food, emitting strangulated gasps.

'Dita ma'am is still here on the campus?' he spluttered.

Heads turned around, staring at him curiously. 'Of course,' came the reply from several voices.

The boy looked at them in acute horror and rushed out of the canteen like a singed cat. Once outside he dialled Arshad Ali's number with a shaking hand. 'Who have you picked up?' he yelled. 'Because it's obviously not Dita Roy. I just verified, she is very much on the campus.'

At that moment, Arshad could have happily killed Utpal; the boy was nowhere to be found when needed, and now he calls with this enlightening piece of information that they have managed to pick up the wrong girl.

So, Arshad wondered, who the fuck was this girl they had picked up?

16

The Godfather

All roads lead to Rome goes the saying, but today was an exception: all paths led to Palash Bose in Phulpukur. He found himself inundated with calls and at the receiving end of volatile recriminations, sentimental tears, furious threats, and barefaced hostility, facing a gamut of emotions in the matter of a few momentous minutes.

It all began with a furious call from Girish Sarkar. 'Palash, I never knew that on top of everything else you are delusional too?'

Palash did not know how to respond to this allegation, so he waited patiently for the follow-up rant. He knew full well that with Girish there was no point in getting into any lines of argument.

'Your incompetent goons have kidnapped Mishti, you know that I suppose? Although for the life of me I can't figure out why, since I had almost offered her to your son on a platter!'

'What?' Palash could not trust his ears. This made no sense.

'Why on earth would I want to kidnap Mishti?' His heart sank to the pit of his stomach as he struggled to figure out probable explanations. Trying to steady the unreasonable tremor of the hand that held the phone, Palash fought to control the waves of panic that threatened to engulf him.

Girish was in no mood to listen to Palash. 'She was on her way to the college because Hemlata had invited her to join her for Bob Banerjee's shoot. Obviously, you and your wife colluded in the kidnapping plan.'

Beside himself with fury, Girish did not let up. 'If you think that you can blackmail me into providing support for your electoral campaigns, I must say this is not the way to do it,' Girish hissed. 'Return my daughter immediately or I will see to it that not only would you not be able to contest for the seat of MLA, I will run a media exposé on you and humiliate you to such an extent that you will never again be able to show your face again in public.'

Intimidated and alarmed, Palash broke out in a cold sweat as he dialled Rajeev's number. Rajeev, meanwhile, was afloat on the floodtide of slogans and banners and protesters shrieking like demented banshees and did not hear Palash's call.

Desperation does strange things to people. When Rajeev did not answer his call, Palash fished out Utpal's number from his phone directory: he had saved Utpal's number just in case he ever needed to get in touch with the leader of the opposition.

Utpal answered immediately. 'Palash kaka, you will not believe what is happening here, it's as if all hell has broken loose and the devil and his infernal company are at the college gate, out to get Dita ma'am.' He sounded as high as a kite.

Palash cut short his histrionics. 'Listen to me carefully, Utpal. I know you were planning to kidnap Dita,' there was a dramatic gasp of surprise at the other end. 'Obviously you could not do so because of the gherao! But then, did you guys abort your plan, or did you crazy fools go ahead and abduct some random girl off the streets?'

Utpal gulped. How had Palash managed to suss out the situation?

'Arshad's boys have picked up a girl. I wasn't there, I have no clue who she is,' he admitted dejectedly.

'You fucking nitwits, you picked up Girish Sarkar's daughter! Tell Arshad he is way out of his depth here. Girish is the godfather of the Diamond Harbour mafia, he will skin you all alive! Return the girl as fast as you can move your miserable arses, do not delay even a minute,' Palash vented his frustration on the flabbergasted boy, who by now was too scared to move, let alone chalk up plans for Mishti's hassle-free return.

Leaving Utpal to figure out how best to tackle the situation, Palash turned his attention to the other calls coming through to him. He noticed he had five missed calls from Pom, he answered the sixth call. 'Where's the fire, Pom?' he struggled to sound casual.

'Everywhere,' came the clipped reply. 'Perhaps you can tell me where Raja is? He hasn't been picking up my calls for a couple of hours. I thought he would be at home.'

Palash chose not to respond to this query, but Pom persisted. 'Ma has been calling him, Papu too, and he has not responded. He doesn't often behave like this!'

Palash's continuing silence made Pom jump to a hasty yet not entirely wrong conclusion. 'You two had a tiff? Why am I not surprised? And don't tell me you've locked him up again. He's not a child any more, you need to grow up, Baba! The last time you did this Raja ran away, you remember? It took us one whole week to find him.'

Raja had always been an errant child, and Palash an impatient parent, and when these two behaved like prize fighters in an arena, it led, more often than not, to unsavoury outcomes. Pom was apprehensive that this might be the scenario unfolding right now, so he recklessly ploughed into the deafening silence.

'I'm already on my way to Phulpukur. Ma called to say she's caught up in some problem at the college; she wants me to pick her up on my way back home. She sounded rather cross with you. Even she hasn't been able to get through to Raja.' Pom's voice took on an almost pleading note, 'Please tell me where Raja is?'

Exasperation, rather than anger, clouded Palash's voice. 'Between you and your mother, you are always ready to assign me the role of the scoundrel in this family. Very convenient for you since you do not have to take hard calls. You leave that to me and then paint me a monster.'

'Baba, that was not my intention. I was worried about Raja's whereabouts myself. I received information from reliable sources that the media, led by the notorious paparazzo Chirag, are desperate to reveal Raja's identity. They have apparently tracked his presence in Phulpukur. And now that Raja has pulled a disappearing trick, I was at a loss as to what to think.'

'Chirag! Oh my God!' Palash could feel his blood pressure shooting up. 'He is indefatigable! He will not give up easily, he will not rest till he gets what he wants. And I still don't know why your stubborn brother wishes not to reveal his identity, I thought he would be quite the preening peacock with his latest round of achievements. What's the need for him to pull a Banksy and create unnecessary intrigue?'

It was Pom's turn to be silent now. Although Raja had always been media-shy, there was no way Pom could tell his father that he was the reason why Raja chose to remain in the shadows, desperate not to spoil his chances with Dita by being associated with Palash.

By now, Palash was breathless with anxiety. 'Are you telling me Chirag Mukherjee is headed towards Phulpukur? That eccentric Bob Banerjee is already prancing around the campus with his crew. Between them they will surely blow up a measly gherao to national levels! We will never be able to live it down. These directors and journos will ruin the reputation of the village as well as the college.'

Pom was completely confused. What is Baba ranting about, he seems to have lost his mind, he thought. 'What have you done? What gherao are you talking about?'

Palash sighed impatiently. 'It's a long story; you will eventually get to know when you pick up your mother, if you can get past the gherao and reach her.' He tossed his phone onto the table and stared at the ceiling. The world and its mother seemed hell-bent on catching up with him. He wondered what he should do now.

17

Guns and Roses

Raja had almost dozed off when he heard the library door rattle open rather noisily. In the doorway, Palash Bose's lanky figure swayed almost like a drunken person. For some unexplained reason, his father had a shotgun in his hands, and it was aimed straight at Raja, albeit somewhat shakily. Raja blinked in confusion and waited for the vision in snow-white dhoti and kurta to disappear. But no matter how much he blinked, the vision did not go away. It kept staring at Raja, mumbling and muttering and finally coming close enough to nudge him with the black muzzle of the gun.

'In my beginning is my end,' Raja quipped, eyeing the gun dispassionately. Truly, the end is here, and it begins and ends with my father, he thought coolly.

Palash was not amused. 'I found out, much to my dismay, that you, my dear son, are the beginning, middle, and end of most of the mayhem that is erupting in my life now. You've led me a merry dance, but I fully intend to end whatever chaos you have set in motion. And this time I will dictate the terms.

'You, who have always stood up against all the plans I make, should not be complaining about being curbed down! It has become a necessity now to control your wayward behaviour!'

'So says the man who has kept his son under lock and key for the past four hours sans food, sans water, sans communication,' drawled the irate son, struggling to control the growing anger that was threatening to consume the last vestiges of respect he had for his father.

'I think I should be the one complaining. First you lock me up and then you come back and point a gun at me like some random goon! If you were not my father, I would have marked you as a madman. What is wrong with you?'

'Wait and watch, you will understand what is wrong with me before this day ends.' Palash replied violently. Then, tossing the keys of his ramshackle Ambassador car towards Raja, who caught them instinctively, he ordered, 'Get up. We are going for a drive.'

Raja had no option but to get up from the sofa where he had just made himself comfortable enough to doze off again. 'Where are we off to, since you obviously will make me drive too?' he jangled the keys.

Palash nudged him with the gun again. 'Hurry up, hurry up! We don't have a moment to lose.'

The gun-toting father pushed the disgruntled son out of the library, frogmarched him along the empty corridors, then chased him down the stairs until he was finally seated in the driver's seat of the Ambassador. 'Drive me to the college,' he barked.

Palash still had the gun trained on Raja, unwilling to brook any signs of resistance. Raja couldn't figure out why his father was pointing the gun at him, but felt relieved that they were headed towards the college and he would be able to see for himself how Dita was handling the gherao. He knew her well enough to assume that she might even talk some sense into Palash to lift the human barricades at the gate.

The distance from the Bose household to Phulpukur College was around seven kilometres, but Palash's Ambassador maintained a slow and steady pace, hence, covering even short distances tended to become a challenge involving inordinate spans of time.

While the chessmen in Raja's mind tried to find a reasonable way out of this fix, Palash was already two moves ahead with his plans. Today was not the day that he intended to be outmanoeuvred by Raja's intransigence and devious schemes.

Holding the gun in one hand, still pointed at Raja, Palash picked up his phone to call Girish. 'I have tracked down your daughter,' he stated without wasting any time on formalities. 'Drive over to the college as soon as you can. Arshad Ali's men had picked her up by mistake, thinking that they were nabbing Dita. They will come back to the college to drop Mishti off, I guess you will want to be there too?' He disconnected abruptly.

Raja was dumbfounded. What the hell is happening? Palash had been up to all kinds of tricks apparently.

'You kidnapped Mishti?' Raja was goggle-eyed with disbelief. 'And planned to kidnap Dita too?'

'Shut up, you fool,' Palash barked. 'I didn't kidnap anyone. Arshad Ali kidnapped Mishti. I am trying to get her back to her father.'

'What about Dita?' Raja asked.

'What about her?' Palash replied absent-mindedly. 'She just creates unnecessary trouble for herself and for me. It was her rash decision to impose restrictions on election posters that led to this entire fiasco.'

Apparently finding it too sensitive a topic to even talk about, Palash adjusted the gun again and answered his phone. Aditya Pundit was on the line, 'Palash, Papu is a bit worried. He cannot seem to reach Raja on his phone. He was wondering if everything's fine?'

'Yes, yes, everything's as fine as can be,' Palash replied impatiently. 'Raja is with me and we are driving down to the college.'

Aditya was immediately concerned, 'Do you think it's wise to interfere in the gherao right now? You will immediately be identified as a Shyamol Sathi sympathizer and considering the fact that this gherao is their brainchild, your association with the party might not work well for your image right now, Palash!'

'My so-called image has gone for a toss, Aditya,' Palash fumed. 'We are all surrounded by dunces, I tell you! Can you imagine some stupid Raktokarobi goons have managed to kidnap Mishti and now Girish Sarkar is threatening me with dire consequences?'

'I know,' commiserated Aditya. 'Sahana is at the college, she just had a conversation with Utpal it seems. Apparently, Arshad Ali had sent goons to pick up Dita. Mishti was simply in the wrong place at the wrong time. Utpal was caught up in the gherao and couldn't leave the campus, hence the entire mix-up. Arshad is livid with anger and wants to have Utpal's head on a platter. He is coming down personally to return the girl. And now, the prospect of being the target of Arshad's wrath has rattled Utpal so much that he has gone and locked himself up in one of the classrooms.'

Palash grunted. 'Utpal should hide himself really well,

since Girish is also on his way to the college. Between Arshad and Girish he might well be caught between the devil and the deep blue sea.'

'You won't believe this, but Utpal had also called Papu, seeking help from Shyamol Sathi, since he is in so much trouble with Raktokarobi head honchos.'

Palash was curious. 'So what did Papu say?'

Aditya hesitated and then blurted out, 'Unfortunately, Papu was so distracted he did not offer any constructive help to Utpal.'

'Why is Papu distracted?' Palash was even more curious.

Aditya hesitated again. 'Papu was concerned about Raja. With Raja being incommunicado, he thought you two might have had a falling out again. You know that Papu has always had a soft spot for Raja, they have literally grown up together.'

The memory of Papu hugging Raja with passionate aplomb in Girish's drawing room flashed across Palash's mind. He shifted uneasily in his seat, hoping against hope that Papu wasn't the special 'someone else' that Raja had mentioned a couple of hours earlier.

Eavesdropping on his father's conversations, some pieces of the puzzle were falling into place for Raja, but there were multiple others that still went unexplained. What mystified him the most was the gun. Raja knew Palash could be recalcitrant, but surely he did not need a gun to drag him out of a room and make him drive his car!

The next snatch of conversation between Palash and Aditya was even more interesting. 'We are driving down to the college,' Aditya informed Palash. 'Radha was feeling rather anxious about Sahana; we will wait for you outside the gates. Pinku and Papu have already left.'

'Can you get me a priest?' Palash asked tersely.

'A priest?' Aditya was flabbergasted, who needs a priest to resolve student politics? Aditya struggled to make sense of this bizarre request. Surely Palash was losing it, he must be under a lot of stress, he thought.

'Yes, a priest,' barked Palash. 'That's who I need to solve all my problems right now.'

Aditya did not know what to say, and in the seat next to Palash, Raja's eyebrows shot up in utter surprise. Trust Baba to come up with out-of-this-world solutions to terribly earthy problems.

Palash's instructions to Aditya were continuing. 'I'm sure you can get hold of Naveen Mukherjee on your way, he has officiated at quite a few Durga pujas and marriages.... He will be able to help me out today.'

'I'll try,' Aditya sounded doubtful. 'But I still don't see how it is going to help us.' As Palash did not seem inclined to reveal his plans, Aditya shrugged and hung up the phone.

18

The Grapes of Wrath

*B*y the time Palash and Raja reached the college, the sky was overcast with storm clouds; the lime green leaves of the Shyamól Sathi banners fluttered jauntily in the powerful gusts of wind. The lazy afternoon had long since retreated into a husk of its former self, anxiety pervaded the air as slogan chanting students surrounded Palash's Ambassador, blocking the ancient vehicle from approaching the college gates.

Palash had no option but to step out of the car and face the belligerent students. Raja turned off the engine and got down after him. The shotgun dangled like a monstrous appendage from Palash's hand and a curious hush descended on the crowd. Instinctively, the crowd stepped back a few paces, shifting away from Palash's menacing figure.

As the milling crowd shifted and regrouped, Raja could see Rajeev's face peeking out of the sea of heads which kept them away from the college gates. He watched with disbelief as Palash snapped his fingers and Rajeev, his greasy hair sticking to his scalp like a grimy cap, came running up to him.

'Palash kaka, we've held the gates as promised,' Rajeev panted, looking askance at the gun. 'There is no need for violence...if Dita ma'am still does not agree to our terms, we will simply prolong the gherao.'

'Nature is planning otherwise, Rajeev.' Palash looked up at the sky, 'A storm is brewing...you won't be able to hold your lines much longer, your supporters will disappear as soon as the rain hits; we have to act fast.'

Immediately aware of the gravity of the situation, Rajeev awaited the action plan that he knew Palash would be rolling out post-haste.

'Ask your boys to open the gates and let us pass, Rajeev,' Palash cast a hooded glance at Raja. 'And take care of this boy, don't let him out of your sight while I try and resolve issues with Dita.'

Whoa, where did this googly come from? Raja was perplexed. By the look of absolute amazement on his face, so was Rajeev: he certainly did not relish the idea of being cast in the role of a babysitter for Raja, while all the action took place elsewhere. But he could not say no to Palash.

Ignoring their surprise, Palash whispered his instructions to Rajeev. 'I can see Pinku and Papu in the crowd, call them over so that they can go in with us. Instruct your student leaders to close the gates securely behind us. They can let in Pom, Aditya, and Girish when they eventually turn up. No one else should be allowed to enter without my permission,' Palash was crystal clear about his instructions. 'Aditya will have a priest in tow, let him enter, he is essential for this evening,' Palash added as a rejoinder.

Pinku and Papu came over to join them, waving enthusiastically and shouting to be heard over the roar of the crowd. Almost instinctively Papu engulfed Raja in a bear hug, conveying silent relief at his deliverance from Palash's clutches.

Palash eyed the exchange with distinct unease, unceremoniously breaking them apart and hurrying them through the gates which were finally opening up for them. Jostling through the crowds, nearly deafened by the triumphant slogans, they managed to enter the campus where someone shoved a Shyamol Sathi banner into Pinku's hands. Pinku struggled to steady the runaway flag in the wind, Palash clutched his gun, and Rajeev kept an iron grip on Raja as the gates closed behind them with a decisive clang.

Meanwhile, all eyes in the principal's office had turned to the college gate. A sudden hush descended on the rowdy crowd, followed by a renewal of excited shouts as the gates started to open. The besieged crowd in the office spotted a few figures stepping inside, one of them waving a flag, and then the gates shut again.

As the figures approached the college enclave, Palash was immediately perceptible. Tall and lithe, dressed in his signature white dhoti and kurta, he cut a figure no one could easily overlook; and today he exuded menace.

'Palash Bose is carrying a gun...the same shotgun he had with him on the wolf hunt,' Dita could hardly believe her eyes. 'Why does he need a gun now?'

I should just have called the police, she thought desperately, instead of listening to Alok. She was quite sure it would only be a matter of time before that gun would be trained on her.

And then she gasped, following Palash's imposing presence, if somewhat unwillingly, was another tall figure... surely that was Raja?

Dita felt a bit out of sorts. Raja had been ignoring her throughout the day, not returning her calls; and then suddenly out of the blue, here he was, that too with Palash Bose?

Beside her, she heard Sahana mumbling, 'Pinku has lost his mind too it seems. Why is he waving the party flag like a demented soul?' she mused, quite cross. What she did not know was that the wind was steadily gathering force and that was the only way Pinku could hold the flag in balance. He dared not dump the banner as Rajeev was keeping a close watch on him too.

Alok and Ashok shook their heads in disapproval. The members of the governing body of the college were flouting norms left, right, and centre: who ever heard of a gun-toting president and a party flag-bearing member?

The teachers and staff who had gathered in Dita's room watched with rapt attention as the tiny group marched resolutely forward.

And then with a slight nod of his head, Palash signalled Rajeev to drag Raja away from the group. Keeping an iron grip on Raja's arm, Rajeev nudged him towards the college canteen. Palash's hands were steady on the gun, he would brook no argument, even Papu's instinctive urge to follow Raja withered under Palash's scornful gaze.

The audience at the office window watched with surprise as the group split, diverging in two directions. Raja was unceremoniously towed away while Palash made his way to the college office.

Raja jerked his arm away from Rajeev. He was still uncertain about his father's plans and in no mood to comply with them. The chessmen in his mind had been shifting around endlessly throughout the day without any conclusive understanding of the situation. Besides, he hadn't been able to communicate with anyone for the last couple of hours to figure out what in the name of hell was actually happening out here.

Rajeev gave him a nasty look. 'No use struggling, you can't run anywhere you know? Those fucking gates out there will only open on my command,' he gloated. The look of supreme satisfaction on the stupid boy's face filled Raja with an instinctive desire to throttle the lad and run for the hills. It was a struggle for Raja to hang on to the last shreds of his sanity.

The atmosphere in the canteen was charged, everyone watched with unabashed curiosity as Raja and Rajeev stepped in through the doors.

Bob and his crew had already run Gopal's stock of tea and biscuits to the ground; Gopal generally took pride in the fact that his canteens both in Phulpukur College and Saint James School were reasonably well stocked, but today everything was spiralling out of control. Some of the people gathered in the canteen were still hungry and were actually raiding the pantry to rustle up some food. All heads swivelled towards Raja and Rajeev as they found an empty table and settled down.

'Here come the scions of the revolution, Inquilab Zindabad,' Bob sniggered, as Gopal jumped out from behind his counter and approached Rajeev.

Thumping his hand on the table in front of Rajeev, Gopal said angrily, 'Inquilab Zindabad my foot! Lads, you have no consideration for the common man, have you?

Staging a gherao at the drop of a hat! And what will the people caught inside eat? Will they fill their stomachs with your empty assurances?'

He turned on Raja too, 'Your father is the source of all this trouble, high time someone taught him a proper lesson.'

'Please go ahead, you have my blessings,' Raja moved away impatiently from the squawking man, his eyes scanning the crowd of faces; his mother was supposed to be here, but he could not spot her. Where could she be?

'You must be looking for Hemlata, I guess,' a gentle voice cut into his thoughts. 'She could not tolerate the crowd around here; Biltu took her to one of the empty classrooms.'

Raja was pleasantly surprised by this unexpected piece of information; apart from this lady with kind eyes who had come over to stand by him, the rest of the crowd in the canteen were literally bristling with hostility. He couldn't blame them really, after a day of hard work everyone had expected to go home when this miserable gherao had upended all their plans. Obviously, Rajeev, being a student leader of Shyamol Sathi, bore the brunt of their hostilities, and Raja was tainted by association.

Raja offered the lady a quick smile of relief, 'Ma finds it painful to be in the company of too many people, she is quite the loner,' he murmured by way of explanation to the graceful woman standing next to him. 'She must have had to rustle up a fair bit of courage to step out to watch you guys shoot, and then getting caught in this political crossfire would have been quite a challenge for her.

'I haven't been able to reach out to her too,' Raja admitted somewhat shamefacedly. 'Baba has set his student goons on me; he took away my phone for good measure and I can't communicate with anyone.'

A sudden look of comprehension dawned on the lady's face, even the crimson of her beautiful bindi appeared animated, 'Oh, was that why Dita was so upset? You did not respond to her calls!'

'Break it up you two,' Rajeev elbowed in into the conversation, rudely nudging past Raja in a physical act of intimidation. Something snapped in Raja's mind: all day long he had been poked and prodded by Palash and could not retaliate, and now this lout of a boy was baiting him in front of a room full of strangers, Raja could endure it no more. He whipped around and landed a resounding slap on Rajeev's cheek, 'High time you learn how to behave, being a student leader does not give you the right to misbehave with people.'

Slack-jawed, Rajeev came up with the most clichéd threat of all time, 'Just you wait till I tell your father.'

'My father does not intimidate me,' Raja laughed recklessly. 'I neither share nor follow his political ideology. You are just a nitwit blindly abiding by his instructions, that much is apparent to me. Go and complain, I don't care.'

'As stubborn as the father,' Rajeev taunted. 'We can bring your entire family down if you don't watch your words.'

Raja charged wildly towards Rajeev, overtaken with blind rage; and then he felt hands holding him back, voices muttering, 'Let him go, he's such a worm, not even worth your anger'; 'Calm down, calm down'; 'Take a deep breath'. Raja felt the anger ebbing out of him as he watched Rajeev beating a hasty retreat out of the canteen door.

Bob Banerjee patted Raja's back approvingly, 'That was well done, lad, I missed a scene worth filming!' he looked towards his crew for endorsement and resounding applause rose like a wave travelling around the room with enthusiastic gusto; it marked the apotheosis of a near villain-like figure into a hero.

Prithvi, Rahul, and Dhruv sidled up next to Bob. 'Just reassuring ourselves that we still have our jobs and haven't been overshadowed by you in Bob's eyes,' they joked as they wove Raja into their convivial circle, trying to ease the stress that was still apparent in Raja's stance.

Raja was grateful for their support, 'I have seen quite a few of your shows with Ma, she is an avid fan. It's crazy, but I seem to know all of you so well.' He turned towards the lady who had offered him unconditional support in an erstwhile hostile crowd, 'I have seen you too, but I can't seem to remember where,' he concluded on a sheepish note.

He could spy the humour twinkling in the eyes of his benefactress. 'Woe is me!' she declared dramatically. 'Everyone knows the charming Dhruv, the handsome Rahul, and the macho Prithvi, but no one pays attention to poor old me.'

Bob laughed out loud, 'Stop being so dramatic woman, you will just confuse the boy,' he turned towards Raja. 'This is Tamali Roy, she is, as you can see, one of our prettiest actresses and definitely the most versatile one.'

The chessmen in Raja's mind started to whirr crazily, jostling around to figure out probable conclusions. 'How did you know Dita was trying to call me? How do you know I ignored her calls?' Grey eyes, brilliant with curiosity, zeroed in on Tamali.

'Why would she not know?' Bob huffed with

exasperation. 'Dita is Tamali's daughter. And between the two of them they share random bits of information that no one else wants to know, much less talk about.'

'Stop pulling my leg, Bob,' Tamali shooed Bob away playfully. 'First get married and then you will understand the trials and tribulations of being a parent.'

'Not in this life, it seems, since you chose Arnab over me!' Bob winked broadly, before he moved away.

Tamali sensed Raja's hooded gaze, trying to figure out just what she knew about him. She hid a smile, biding her time. The red bindi on her forehead sparkled with mischief, she couldn't let go of the chance to tease this secretive boy. Just a little bit!

'In case you are wondering exactly what I know about you, let me assure you I know much more about you than Dita does,' Tamali pepped up her words with a semi-wicked smile. 'I know all about you Anuraj Bose; and I am wondering what to do with the information.'

Jeez, thought Raja, here comes the axe. Just my luck to be ironed out by Dita's mother in front of a room full of strangers. And most of them seemed to be gaping at them, all agog to participate in the drama that was unfolding in front of their eyes.

'What I don't understand, Anuraj Bose, is why this secrecy? You are quite famous?' Tamali persisted.

'Anuraj Bose!' Bob wheeled around and jumped back. 'You don't say?' He gaped at Raja, poking a curiosity laden finger at Raja's chest. 'This boy is Anuraj Bose... chess prodigy?'

'Stop jabbing at him, Bob,' Tamali scolded. 'Next thing I know you will poke a hole into him.'

Raja had never been cornered and questioned so boldly. 'It's a long story,' he offered lamely, trying to sidle out of the range of Bob's poking fingers.

'Since we are really not going anywhere, we have all the time in the world,' Tamali settled down on one of the canteen chairs. 'Do tell us your story, Anuraj.'

Oh boy! No escape today, Raja moaned in silent despair.

To exacerbate matters even further, Bob had fished out his phone and was shouting into it at the top of his lungs. 'You were looking for Anuraj Bose, were you not? You won't believe me, but I have him here!' He paused for a second, listening intently. 'You are already on your way to Phulpukur? Wonderful, come up to the college as soon as you get there. There's a small demonstration happening at the gate, but I think you can play the media card and just enter?'

Satisfied with the way the conversation went, Bob finally settled down beside Raja to hear his story.

'Who did you just call?' Raja sounded jittery, his tall frame stiff with tension. 'Someone from the media?'

'Chirag Mukherjee,' Bob offered casually. 'He's a good friend of mine. Only last week he was bemoaning the fact that Anuraj Bose had given him the slip again and he badly wanted to do an interview with him. That's why I called him,' Bob sounded extremely pleased with himself.

Raja groaned. Grey eyes flooded over with panic.

'Bob,' Tamali was shocked, her heart went out to Raja. 'Anuraj is famous in his own right, he does not need Chirag to validate him.'

Too late, thought Raja, too late. His personal life would be up for grabs now, they were coming at him with searchlights on, waiting to chase him out of the shadows he had crafted around himself.

'May I borrow your phone?' he requested, instinctively reaching out to Tamali. 'I need to call Pom.'

19

Things Fall Apart

*T*he college gates opened again, to let in another gun-toting individual. This time it was Girish, with his gun trained at Arshad Ali, who had mistakenly assumed that by returning Mishti personally to Girish he might avert the furious man's wrath. Obviously, he was horribly wrong, as was evident in the way he was being pushed and prodded by Girish. Mishti, now free, watched with unabashed glee as her father directed Arshad towards the principal's office. Jai brought up the rear of this motley group; he too had a gun as he had come prepared to fight to free Mishti from the Raktokarobi goons.

The atmosphere in Dita's room thrummed with tension; Palash and Dita had reached an impasse and neither of them seemed inclined to give up an iota of control. When Girish entered with Arshad, intimidation dynamics tilted a bit more towards the men with guns and shifted abysmally out of the orbit of the ones who did not have weapons, but only raw, foolhardy courage. The latter group included Dita.

Girish did not mince his words as he shoved Arshad into the room. 'Palash, look how your grand plans have misfired! What do you want to do now?'

An infuriated Palash pointed a shaking finger at Arshad, 'This oaf's intention was to threaten and intimidate Dita, to coerce her to sanction electoral posters on college walls. But obviously, his minions being nothing but brainless wretches, they picked up the wrong girl.'

'I know that, but ultimately you are the person responsible for setting things in motion, and you are responsible for the dreadful mess which is unfolding,' Girish stopped Palash with a smouldering look. 'It's time to wrap up the chaos you have unleashed.'

A glimmer of irony lit up Dita's otherwise miserable day: the guns were now trained away from her, and two of the wiliest of men were at each other's throat now. She even found it in herself to be somewhat glad about the gherao, otherwise she would surely have been kidnapped and God only knows what could have unfolded after that. At least, in the gherao she was on familiar ground, with known people. One had to be thankful for the small mercies of life.

Both Palash and Girish had their guns trained on Arshad now. Dita hoped they would not do anything foolish, with the world and its mother as audience, so ignoring all laws of self-preservation which should have held her back, she jumped into the fray.

'Arshad might be foolhardy, but don't forget, he too is a product of your stupid electoral politics where people like him actually think that putting up posters on a wall—or not being able to do so—can summarily lead to a case of kidnapping and resolution through intimidation. Goon politics at its best!'

Trying to reason with the two irate men, Dita continued, 'All's well that ends well, is it not? The kidnapping was an obviously botched attempt. The best thing you can do is lodge a complaint with the police. Let him go now.

'And call off the gherao,' she added wearily.

While the attention of the two men was somewhat distracted by Dita, Arshad had started to move slyly towards Palash; he knew that of the two, Palash wasn't really a pro with guns. Arshad had decided to take the chance of wresting it out of his hands. Bracing himself for the only fallback plan he could think of, he lunged towards Palash.

Palash was caught unawares. Near-blinded with anger at Dita's words, he had failed to notice Arshad's movements. When Arshad lunged, Palash nearly jumped out of his skin and pulled the trigger of the shotgun in an unpremeditated response. There was a loud bang and he staggered from the recoil; he dimly registered people around him frozen in a terrible moment of suspense as the bullet sought its victim.

Arshad jumped back with a startled shriek. The bullet found its mark, hit an unsuspecting target, and made him crash with a resounding thud, landing on the office floor with very little dignity or grace.

For a few seconds everything froze and then all hell broke loose. What the bullet had brought down was Durjoy Pundit's portrait from its prized position up on the wall. The colossal frame splintered into smithereens, hitting the ground right next to where Mishti was standing; a mere inch here or there and she could have been a dead duck.

While Palash and Girish seemed to have turned to stone with shock, Alok and Dipten grabbed a kicking, cussing Arshad and dragged him out of the room before he could cause more mischief.

Poor Durjoy Pundit lay in disgrace on the floor; Pinku and Papu pushed people out of the way and began to pick up the pieces of the frame that had held the portrait of their infamous grandfather. Dita and Sahana tried to help them as much as they could. Mishti appeared shell-shocked and sidled in beside her father. Girish hugged his daughter in a rare moment of parental reassurance.

Palash's hands were still shaking when Aditya Pundit entered the room with a stranger in tow. The sight that met his eyes wasn't something he was expecting. While Durjoy was spreadeagled on the floor for some obscure reason, Pinku, Papu, and Sahana seemed to be gathering pieces of splintered wood, Palash and Girish were obviously at loggerheads, and most of the teachers and staff seemed to be in a state of shock.

What was even more intriguing was the way in which Dita was down on bended knees, trying to gather bits of the broken frame, totally oblivious to the fact that both Palash and Girish had trained their guns on her now.

'I agree with you, Palash,' Girish muttered. 'This girl is at the heart of all the troubles erupting here.'

Dita looked up, saw that she was the target of two guns, resigned herself to her fate, and settled herself on the floor. She could sense Sahana, Pinku, and Papu closing in beside her in a silent gesture of solidarity. No one knew what would happen next.

Aditya was perplexed and angry, he could not control himself any longer. 'What exactly is happening here? Why has my father's portrait been taken off the wall? Why are my sons being held at gunpoint?'

'Your sons are not being held at gunpoint,' Palash hissed. 'Ask them to move away and let me deal with Dita.'

Pinku and Papu seemed to be in no mood to heed the elders. Sahana did not let go of her hold on Dita; they held themselves together in stubborn defiance.

Palash nodded at the stranger who had entered with

Aditya, distinctly out of place. He was a thin and bony man with a sacred thread, the upavita, crossing his bare torso diagonally, drifting down his left shoulder in wisps of brilliant white, a tuft of hair, longer than the rest, dangled at the back of his head, with a wilting marigold blossom tied to it.

'Naveen Mukherjee, I presume?' Palash asked.

'Yes,' Aditya answered curtly, he did not like the way Palash was taking matters into his own hands.

Girish, too, was puzzled, 'Naveen is our local priest, why would you want him here now, Palash?'

'He can solve many of my problems and yours as well, Girish,' Palash was cryptic. 'There is only one way for us to deal with our troublemakers.' He turned his attention to the teachers who were huddled up in small groups, 'Agni and Utpal can go to the canteen and bring Raja here. Alok, Biltu, and Ashok clean up the assembly hall and let Naveen Mukherjee set up a small mandap.'

Agni left the room, muttering under his breath; he had no idea who Raja was, but was too scared to admit this to the two crazy men with guns. He dragged Utpal with him in the hope that whatever happened, Utpal would share the same fate.

The world outside was in a state of meltdown: the strong winds had stopped and given way to a torrential downpour. The Shyamol Sathi banners drooped and dangled, beaded with moisture, the belligerence of the protesting students had been driven back, liquefied by the tumultuous assault of nature. Abandoning their posts and party banners, they ran helter-skelter; a few of them stopped to open up the college gates before disappearing into the sleety rain which engulfed everything.

20

Catch Me If You Can

Chirag Mukherjee was in a fix. He tapped his fingers in frustration against the cold steely surface of his laptop, staring out blindly at the rain-washed world from inside his Toyota Corolla, his oaken jaw rigid with frustration, his hawkish nose twitching with evident distaste as he took stock of the mud and slime around his car.

Chirag, armed with the grim determination of a true-blue journalist, had set out on a wild goose chase with two members of his journalistic team to locate Anuraj Bose; his hunch had been validated by Bob's call, but now, almost near Phulpukur, his car had stalled.

Satyajit and Badal, the two young journalists accompanying him, were already so overworked that Chirag could not find it in his heart to ask them to step out into the pelting rain to check what was wrong with the car. He switched on the hazard lights, curled his lanky frame into the comfort of the soft leather, sighing as he took off his horn-rimmed glasses and closed his weary eyes, readying himself for an interminable wait on this godforsaken village road.

After nearly one-and-a-half hours, which passed in silent misery chomping on the last few sleeves of Oreo cookies that they had with them, a car pulled up by their side and the driver rolled down his window. Chirag did the same, shouting at the top of his voice against the turbulence to make the stranger understand his predicament. The stranger nodded and gestured to Chirag to join him in his car. Soon, the three thoroughly drenched journalists and the stranger were on their way to Phulpukur again.

Chirag, having secured the seat next to the driver, tried ineffectively to wipe the moisture from his face and offered the stranger an impish smile, 'Can't thank you enough dude, you are a lifesaver.'

The stranger smiled enigmatically. 'Chirag Mukherjee, if I am not wrong? You are on your way to Phulpukur College?'

Chirag was a bit taken aback; his was a familiar face on national television, so no wonder the stranger recognized him, but how did he know he was on his way to Phulpukur College?

Chirag chose to remain silent. The stranger laughed, 'It's no secret that you are chasing Anuraj! He warned me that you were on your way to the college after Bob supplied all the information you needed.'

Pom laughed again at Chirag's perplexed expression, 'I am Anuraj's brother, Anupam. I know you have been chasing him all over the place and you know what, I think finally he has come to terms that he cannot hide his identity because of busybodies like you.'

Chirag nodded sagely, concurring with Pom's opinion. 'But we have to be busybodies, you know, in our profession we have to be inquisitive, cannot help it,' he shrugged. 'If I don't reveal Anuraj's identity, someone else does, it's as simple as that.'

The heavy rain made for poor visibility and Pom had to concentrate on the roads, conversation dipped, and the rest of the journey was completed in uneasy silence.

By the time they reached the college, the rain had successfully driven away the student protesters, a few abandoned banners lay on the college grounds in muddy desolation. The gates were wide open, and Pom drove in, taking the car as close as possible to the canteen as that was where he knew Raja would be. That was where Raja had asked him to come.

The four of them jumped out of the car. Pom made a mad dash towards the canteen doors and the other three followed his lead blindly. In the grey evening light, through sheets of rain, Pom could make out two more figures ahead of him, making a beeline towards the canteen. And then, suddenly, the lights around them began to flicker and fail, the wind gathered even more force, and the world plunged into a deep, damp darkness.

Moving forward instinctively, staggering and stumbling, drenched to the skin, the four of them managed to reach the canteen; Bob's crew had already switched on the torches of their phones and in the curious play of shadow and light, Pom could see that the two figures ahead of him had also reached the canteen, dripping all over the place. One of them called out in a stentorian voice, 'Can Raja please step out? We have been asked to take him to the assembly hall.'

Agni appeared ill at ease having to shout like this, as it is he was half blind in the darkness and doubly disadvantaged because he had never seen or met Raja.

Pom stopped short, holding Chirag back, because both of them had spotted Raja in the gloom which surrounded a group at the back of the room. Chirag followed Pom's cue with commendable ease, not giving any indication that he knew where Raja was. Curiously, nor did anyone from the crowd, a strange hush seemed to have descended on the room, broken only by the sound of the interminable rain.

'Why do you want Raja?' Bob's voice boomed in the darkness. 'Why should he go to the assembly hall?'

Pom stepped up, 'More to the point, who sent you guys? What's happening in the hall?'

Agni did not know how to address all these queries at once; behind him, Utpal shuffled his feet, thoroughly intimidated by the restless crowd that surrounded them. Irritated by the wild goose chase they had been sent on, Agni wanted to get it over and done with as soon as possible. 'I don't know exactly what is going on, but Palash Bose has called for a priest and the office staff are currently setting up a mandap in the college hall. Aditya Pundit brought the priest with him and Girish Sarkar is there too, with his daughter.'

'And Palash Bose sent us here to find Raja,' Utpal added.

Hidden in the shadows at the back of the room, Tamali had been following the conversation with avid interest; suddenly she felt Raja, who was standing next to her, stiffen with shock. She turned towards him with undisguised concern, he was mumbling something inaudible under his breath.

The chessmen finally fell into position, Raja could now see very clearly what Palash planned to do; the props were all there, the shotgun to put him in place, the priest to marry him off, to whom? To Mishti?

Agni was still blinking to adjust his vision in the dark. 'We need Raja to walk back to the hall with us,' his voice sounded almost apologetic.

Tamali could barely make out Raja muttering under his breath, 'Oh no! Oh no!' His grey eyes had gone dark with panic, blinded by the darkness, and feeling trapped. Barely understanding what was happening, Tamali caught Prithvi's eyes and a silent decision was taken.

Prithvi stepped forward, masked in darkness, with a few faltering beams from cell phone torches following him. 'Come, let's go and finish this business,' he sneered at Agni. 'I am Raja.'

The crowd gaped at the blatant lie; however, sensing that something dark and dangerous must be afoot, everyone decided to keep quiet. Tamali winked at Raja. Enjoying the drama of the moment, Bob prodded Agni to take quick action, 'Get on with it, take Raja and let us all go home.'

Chirag, in the meantime, was finding it difficult to control his laughter, as a thoroughly confused Agni and Utpal led Prithvi away. Gopal shoved an umbrella into Prithvi's hands, disdainfully ignoring the other two miserable wretches.

Once they disappeared into the darkness outside the doors, Chirag made a beeline towards Raja, followed by Satyajit and Badal. Even from a distance Pom could make out that Raja's face was pale with fatigue, but today the world was catching up with him, and there seemed to be no escape.

'Till now it has been a game of catch me if you can with you,' Chirag could not hide the smugness in his voice. 'But I have finally managed to pin you down! So, let me ask you why this cat and mouse chase? You have achieved international fame at such a young age, why this curious desire to stay in the shadows like a hermit?'

Satyajit's camera was ready; the long-evaded interview

was about to begin.

'Wait, wait, wait,' Bob hollered. 'The boy is looking positively wan, you cannot put him up on national television looking like this.' Within seconds of this astute observation two hands from Bob's make-up crew managed to make Raja look somewhat presentable.

Resigned to his fate, Raja faced the camera, taking his time to answer Chirag; Pom watched from afar, talking to Hemlata on the phone. 'You will not believe this, Ma. Raja is being interviewed by Chirag Mukherjee and Bob is filming the interview. For someone who chose to lie low, his cover is being blown sky high, and how!

'Meanwhile, Father is trying to marry him off to Mishti, perhaps you can do something to stop this madness?' Hemlata could not believe her ears: while she had been waiting for the gherao to get over, the world seemed to have tilted on its axis and Palash was striding over it like an angel of doom. 'Where is this marriage going to take place, Pom?' she croaked, and then listened intently to Pom's conjectures. A few minutes later she was limping towards the assembly hall with Biltu in tow.

21

Heart of Darkness

A large space had been hastily cleared by the college staff in the assembly hall. Chairs and benches were stacked together helter-skelter on the fringes as Naveen Mukherjee, his upavita now wound around his ears, shouted out his orders to construct the makeshift mandap.

Palash and Girish, still enjoying the gun-toting mafia image, had managed to gather the rest of the staff together in the hall, nudging the recalcitrant Papu and Pinku, and the fuming Dita and Sahana into grudging submission, while Mishti and Aditya followed despondently.

Rajeev, after being berated soundly by Palash, hung around by the door, keeping an eye on things so that Arshad did not find his way back to create further trouble. It was then that he saw two soggy figures step out of the rain. In the darkness he could barely recognize them as Agni and Utpal; striding ahead of them, relatively dry, was a staggeringly handsome man—it was Prithvi. Rajeev wondered what they were up to.

Completely ignoring Rajeev, Prithvi rushed into the hall, followed by a panting Agni and Utpal. Furious at being brushed aside so peremptorily, Rajeev caught hold of Utpal, 'Why have you brought Prithvi here?'

Utpal blinked, 'Prithvi? Who is Prithvi? We have Raja with us!'

Rajeev and Utpal looked at each other, hooded glances cloaked in utter confusion.

Out of the corner of his eye, Rajeev registered a sudden swerve in Prithvi's stride, he seemed to be heading to the rear of the hall. Rajeev looked around and saw a few figures slumped on chairs just behind the mandap. Obviously, Prithvi had recognized someone there.

The confusion at the gate had captured Palash's attention, he was perplexed to see a strange young man charge into the room, followed by Agni. Palash snapped his fingers and Agni came running up to him. 'We finally managed to get Raja!' he gloated.

Palash narrowed his eyes in disdain. 'Where?' came the clipped query.

Taken aback, Agni pointed at Prithvi, who seemed to be involved in an intense conversation with the occupants of the chairs beyond the mandap.

'Who is he?' Palash hissed. 'That's not Raja.'

While Agni's eyes seemed to be popping out of their sockets, Girish came to the rescue. 'That young man over there is Prithvi, one of the main leads in Bob's web series.' Agni gaped. It took him a moment to process this information before coming to the grudging conclusion that he had been royally duped.

Girish took Palash aside, 'I still don't know what you are trying to do here, Palash,' his voice was laced with concern. 'But if you are trying to marry Mishti off to your boy without his consent, you will have me to answer to. I will not have my daughter dumped on unwilling candidates. She is far too precious to me to be treated with such cursory disregard.'

Palash sighed, 'Believe me, Mishti has never been a part of my plans here, even her kidnapping has been totally accidental. I needed to clip the root of all my troubles at its base, and you know that Dita has been the bone of contention for a long time now. Let me deal with it my way, but I will need you by my side.'

Girish nodded in silent sympathy; he had no qualms about siding with Palash as long as his own interests were not hurt.

Palash summoned Rajeev, rattling off a series of instructions as the boy came up to him. 'Take these two fools,' he pointed at Agni and Utpal, 'go to the canteen, get hold of everyone and bring them here.'

Rajeev appeared a bit unsure. 'There are droves of people in the canteen, and last time they just hooted me out of the place, why would they listen to me now?'

'Because you have this,' Palash handed over his shotgun to Rajeev. 'If you really think you need numbers to intimidate the crowd, take Utpal and Arshad with you, along with Jai, he too has a gun. Let's see if Utpal and Arshad can redeem themselves by cleaning up the mess they have created.'

Rajeev held the gun sheepishly, pleased to imagine that he would finally cut a figure of authority. Girish brought him back to earth with a harsh rejoinder, 'Don't be a fool and shoot it off to prove a point, else the rest of your life you will be behind bars in a miserable jail.'

Rajeev looked peeved and left the hall with Jai and Agni, all of whom looked extremely unhappy at the prospect of being drenched to the skin in the unrelenting rain yet again.

The figures huddled into a group behind the mandap

watched the handover of the gun in uneasy silence, and then looked at each other.

'Whatever is going on, we are in for a rough patch,' Papu muttered. 'What I don't understand is why they brought you here, Prithvi?'

Prithvi averted his gaze from Mishti, who was looking at him with such unabashed admiration that even he felt embarrassed. 'Two oafs had been sent to nab Raja,' he explained. 'Obviously they did not know Raja from Adam. So, I played a practical joke.'

'Tamali appeared a bit concerned for Raja,' Prithvi continued seriously. 'I think I picked up SOS signals from her. I really don't know what it was that was worrying her,' he explained, catching the wary look in Dita's eyes as he mentioned her mother's name.

Dita was still cross with Raja for not having reached out to her all through the long and miserable day. 'God only knows what he has told Mom to make her so concerned. A couple of hours back they did not even know each other,' she confided morosely to Sahana, who was seated next to her.

Pinku, who had overheard Dita, chipped in with his observations. 'Have you wondered why Naveen Mukherjee has set up the mandap? I think we are headed for a shotgun marriage, but since no one appears to be pregnant or otherwise here, why is this even happening?'

All eyes turned to Mishti. 'Is your father trying to marry you off to Raja? Is that why Raja's presence here is so important?' Sahana asked.

As Mishti was vociferously denying Sahana's allegations, Dita's heart sank; she knew Palash Bose would stop at nothing. She picked up her phone to call her mother.

Tamali answered the call but a barrage of background chatter made it near impossible for Dita to hear anything. Shouting over the din, Dita asked, 'What exactly is happening in the canteen, Mom? It's so noisy!'

Tamali shouted back, 'Chirag Mukherjee is interviewing Raja, and the live audience that we have here is going crazy with excitement.'

Dita's head was spinning. She could not figure out why Chirag Mukherjee of all people would want to interview Raja. She was flummoxed.

Tamali's voice descended to a whisper, 'I can't speak too loudly because the recording is on, but my heart is going out to the poor boy, being chased to the ends of the earth by Chirag and apparently being forced by his father to marry some girl.'

Dita felt faint. She realized she had not eaten throughout the day and the tension and anxiety were finally catching up with her. 'Who does his father want him to marry? Who is his father, have you met him?' she whispered back.

Dita thought she spotted guilty looks on Pinku and Sahana's faces, but she was too focused on Tamali's words to pay them any attention.

'I think he wants Raja to marry Mishti, to fulfil some political obligations,' Tamali whispered back, and then suddenly her voice rose to a piercing shriek, 'Oh my God! Oh my God! That stupid boy is back with a gun....' Tamali's voice petered out into deafening silence. The line went dead.

Dita went numb with disbelief. 'I think Raja's father wants him to marry Mishti,' she mumbled. Nothing seemed to make sense any more, it was as if she was stuck in a maze, blindsided even by Raja.

Papu and Pinku looked at each other, overcome by the anguish of not being able to divulge so many essential facts. But the secrets were not theirs to reveal, they would have to leave it all to Raja, they decided.

'Why is Raja being interviewed by Chirag Mukherjee?' Dita wondered aloud. Sahana opened her mouth to explain, but was immediately silenced by Pinku's glance.

Mishti, on the other hand, found it riveting, 'Chirag Mukherjee is the god of national television,' she declared dramatically. 'I just might agree to marry Raja if Chirag covers our marriage on national TV. This girl is ready for the shotgun marriage.'

All five pairs of eyes pinned her down with silent reprimand, and then Papu broke the uneasy silence with his own personal brand of humour. 'I think I had staked my claim on Raja way ahead of you, Mishti, and he would choose me over you any given day.'

The ensuing laughter brought the tension down by a few notches, but Dita was still agitated as she wondered how her mother was dealing with Rajeev and his goons in the canteen. Observing her gloomy expression Prithvi came over and sat down by her side. 'Don't worry, Tamali knows how to handle difficult situations. But the challenge here is Rajeev and the gun, I hope that fool doesn't do anything stupid. Might not be an easy thing to do with so much media coverage too!'

By now, Prithvi had secured Dita's undivided attention. 'I don't understand why Raja is emerging as the magnet for media attention. What am I missing here?'

At the back of her mind, an intriguing memory seemed to float up from her subconscious—Raja's uncharacteristic and unexplained haste at the airport when she had gone to receive him, his hasty attempts to divert her attention from media personnel who appeared to be chasing him. Pieces of the puzzle that had worried her since then, finally seemed to be coming together.

She looked at Prithvi, seeking an explanation, demanding it in silence; and Prithvi gave in. 'I think Raja is a chess prodigy of some sort! I don't know much about chess, but from what Bob said I gathered that Raja's claim to fame is both at national and international levels. And that is why Chirag Mukherjee is so desperate to interview him.'

Dita's mind went blank. This revelation was greater than anything she had ever expected, her Tea Boy was a chess champion. And he had never let her know. The moment of joy was punctured by gloom once again: perhaps he did not want her in his life after all. Otherwise, why this immense cover-up? He just wanted to please his father and marry Mishti. She herself was just a temporary fling.

Another conversation from the seemingly distant past kept buzzing around in her mind; Tamali had talked about a chess player from Phulpukur.... For the life of her Dita could not remember the man's name but felt sure that it wasn't Raja.

'Maybe you should just marry Raja and be done with it, Mishti,' Dita rounded on Mishti with uncharacteristic grumpiness. 'I am sure that is what Palash and Girish have been planning to achieve throughout this painful day.'

Palash and Girish watched with surprise as a visibly angry Dita marched up to them. 'You two have been up to all kinds of tricks; first the problem with political posters, then the gherao and the foolhardy kidnapping, and now a preposterous marriage. Enough is enough, we are not going to sit around all day waiting for this wedding to happen. You have my blessings, go ahead and get Raja married off to Mishti, but let us go home now!'

Girish jumped into the fray with considerable enjoyment. 'I will never allow Mishti to marry Raja like this! It is out of the question.'

Dita was so embarrassed, she did not know where to look, and Palash seemed absolutely delighted by her discomfiture. The uneasy silence stretched on and on and on, until Hemlata tackled Palash, 'I heard you are planning to marry Raja off to Mishti? Are you out of your mind?. Did you even wait for his consent? I'm telling you he will run away again; besides, I will not have my son married off like this! He is not a toy that you can hand over to this man in your quest for political power,' she glared at Girish, making him squirm like a worm under a probing microscope.

Peals of laughter, shrill and hysterical, buzzed around in Dita's head. Here we go again and again and again, she thought.

22

The Marriage of Heaven and Hell

*A*ditya had spent the last hour trying to reassemble the portrait of his infamous ancestor. Coming to terms with the fact that it was quickly becoming an exercise in futility, he finally ripped it out of the remnants of the frame and rolled it into a scroll. He was determined that Durjoy should be a part of whatever ceremony was about to take place in the assembly hall: it was only fair that the founder member of the college should be present for important events.

As he stepped out of the principal's office, a curious sight met his eyes. Shadowy figures, doused in darkness and rain, emerged into the corridors where the office staff had placed a few candles. In the flickering candlelight, Aditya could make out that a small crowd was being prodded to move forward by Rajeev, who for some unexplained reason had a gun trained on the miserable drenched figures.

They moved towards the entrance of the hall. As if in a trance, Aditya followed.

Someone in the crowd was creating a commotion. Aditya recognized the voice—it was the voice that made a racket on national television during the evening news hours. Chirag was indeed protesting vociferously. With rainwater dripping down his hair, sliding into his eyes and nose, nearly blinding him in the darkness, he sounded distinctly whiny, but no one seemed to be paying him any attention.

The commotion at the hall door immediately attracted the attention of those within. Palash's eyebrows shot up as he realized that in his haste to corner Raja he had ordered a bona fide circus to flood the hall. He watched with wary resignation as Bob's crew crept in grumbling and irritable. Chirag continued his rant, oblivious of his surroundings, hanging on to Raja like a limpet, as if he was afraid that Raja would vanish again if let loose. A disgruntled Pom followed with Utpal and Agni, drenched to the skin and shivering. Their footsteps left puddles of water in their wake, and Aditya, who brought up the rear end of the group, had to skip across the puddles to reach Palash and Girish.

Dita's eyes met Raja's. He was looking positively piqued but considering the fact that he had gone to such lengths to conceal high points of his life from her, she was not in the mood to feel any sympathy for him. She averted her eyes, looking for Tamali in the crowd.

Palash snapped his fingers and Rajeev ran up to him with all the obedience of a trained dog. The gun changed hands. Jai walked up with his gun, guarding Palash and Girish with dogged perseverance.

Observing Rajeev's intense desire to please Palash, Pom wondered whether this was the kind of blind faith Palash sought from his errant sons. And having failed to achieve this, had he turned feral in his rage, especially over his complete inability to control Raja? Pom failed to find any trace of sanity in a situation where three guns were holding so many people at ransom, subject to the whims and fancies of two mad men.

But both men were wily and methodical. Following their

instructions Rajeev, Utpal, and Arshad had systematically divested everyone of their cell phones; all connection to the external world was now well and truly broken and there was no chance of Diamond Harbour police attempting to reach out to them in the tumultuous rain.

The hall was now lit only by the flames of dozens of flickering candles and the tension in the air was so thick that it could literally be cut with a sharp knife. The menacing presence of the guns had managed to silence Chirag and Bob, and the crowd waited with trepidation.

The guns moved to find their targets, the one in Girish's hand pointed straight at Raja. The crowd gasped. The one in Palash's hands had also found its mark, unerringly trained on Dita. The crowd went still, broken only by a soft cry— Tamali had fainted.

Dita froze in disbelief. What exactly did Palash want?

Girish stepped forward, nudging Raja towards the mandap with his gun. A look of utter incomprehension descended on Raja's face, why was the other gun trained at Dita?

Girish offered Raja a sickening smile, 'This is Palash's solution to the current problems. Both of you are constant irritants to his political aspirations, so he wants to curb Dita's challenges by forcing her into a disadvantageous marriage with a virtual stranger; in this case, it is you!

'It's a good thing for me too,' Girish continued, as he pushed Raja forward. 'With you out of contention, Pom and Mishti might still have a better chance at marriage themselves.'

Raja was intrigued by this explanation. He heard someone in the crowd sniggering and realized it was Pom, trying to control his laughter. It was a bizarre turn of events, measures meant to create chaos, leading to instinctive harmony.

Dita, however, was incandescent with anger, her face flaming like a furnace. 'How dare you think that you can marry me off to a random stranger like a common trollop?'

'Trollop,' Chirag murmured, edging closer to the mandap. 'Satyajit, take note, this is a new word, an addition to my vocabulary.' Satyajit ignored him, there was no way he could actually take note in the flickering darkness.

Sensing the high drama that was surely about to unfold, Chirag tried to sidle up as close as possible to Raja, fishing out from the depth of his soggy pocket the second phone he habitually carried, the one that Palash's goons hadn't been able to find. He put it on video mode and waited for an opportune moment; hoping that the goons would be too distracted with the drama unfolding in front of their eyes to pay him any attention.

With deadly calm, Palash addressed Dita. 'Don't you think you've thrown your inane challenges at me too many times? And constantly hoped that I would digest your insolent attitude in silence and look the other way while you continue to do whatever you think best? Well, now it is pay-up time.' He moved towards her, forcing her towards the mandap.

Naveen Mukherjee's exertions throughout the evening were finally being vindicated, but he had mixed feelings regarding this ceremony. In his long career as a priest, he had never before married off people held at gunpoint. Was it even legal, he wondered, a shotgun marriage in this day and age? But being far too scared of Girish and Palash to question their motives, he started mumbling the mantras, shaking inside his skeletal frame, his mind like a wayward leaf, aflutter on waves of anxiety.

Hemlata, however, was not to be cowed down so easily, she had very little faith in the rationality of Palash's motives. 'You are making her pay by marrying her off to Raja? What has the boy done to deserve such a fate?' she objected, while Tamali who had regained consciousness but looked pale and shell-shocked, watched glumly.

Dita's temper shot up like a rocket again. 'I don't believe this! You are actually implying that I will be the bane of his existence if he marries me? Marrying me is some form of punishment? Who wants to marry him anyway?'

If looks could kill, Raja would have been half-dead by now. 'And by the way, I've heard that his father wants him to marry Mishti. So, move that stupid gun away from my face. I am not in the mood to marry anyone here.'

Palash was baffled, 'His father?' He looked around him for some reasonable explanation, unable to process the fact that Dita still did not know that Raja was his son. 'Who do you think is his father?'

Raja blanched: here comes the grand exposé, Dita would never forgive him now. What should have been revealed to her very delicately, in private, would now be rudely announced in front of all the world.

Raja closed his eyes and waited.

Dita was puzzled at Palash's query. 'How would I know? I did not even know until now that he is a so-called chess prodigy.'

She was blindingly aware of this lapse from her side, disregarding the necessity to delve deeper into Raja's identity! Had she talked herself into a willing suspension of disbelief?

Had it subconsciously struck her that his identity might be a difficult cross to bear?

She did not even know Raja's full name. I have just built my own narrative around my Tea Boy, she mused. A fable, a myth, a figment of the imagination.

Shaking her head to clear her mind, Dita wondered why Sahana and Pinku had stricken expressions plastered on their faces as they stood at the periphery of the mandap. They must know something that I don't, Dita concluded; was there no end to this confusion? And then she saw her mother with a glazed expression, her red bindi throbbing like an open wound on her ashen face; was she hiding something too?

Chirag could not control himself any longer, the ensuing silence was killing him. Risking the guns and the two mad men, he elbowed his way closer to the mandap, launching into a dramatic narrative of events that were unfolding right in front of his eyes. 'The nation has been wanting to know this for a long time! Who is Anuraj Bose, the talented young man who has managed to defeat the grandmasters of chess with consummate ease? Over the last few years, he has managed to evade the media, keeping his identity under wraps. But today we have managed to uncover him at last, and what an occasion it is, as it seems he is about to get married, or is being forced to get married.'

Bob watched Chirag in action with a grudging sense of appreciation: he had to give it to the man, he refused to be intimidated by the gunmen in his elemental desire to report breaking news. Bob signalled a few of his crew members, who had smuggled in cameras under waterproof wraps, to join Chirag.

Chirag panned his phone, rolling on the video mode

to a close-up shot of Dita's face, rattling off questions at supersonic speed, 'Are you glad that you are marrying Anuraj Bose, the latest chess prodigy on the block? Do you have any idea of the scope and span of his achievements at such a young age? Or are you just being forced to marry him? Do you know him personally or is this the first time that you are meeting him, that too, ironically, on the occasion of your marriage? But before we evaluate the dynamics of the situation, can you please introduce yourself to our audience?'

'Anuraj Bose,' Dita repeated to herself, looking straight at Raja, that was the name Tamali had mentioned so long ago, Raja was Anuraj, and she had never, in her wildest dreams, made the connection.

Raja looked back in silence, a silent plea for understanding shimmering in his eyes, grey hovering on midnight black, clouding over with trepidation as he realized Dita was finding it difficult if not impossible to deal with the situation.

And then it struck her like a bolt of lightning—Anuraj Bose was Palash Bose's son! She gagged on the thought, suffocating under its nightmarish implications. A feeling of distaste choked her sensibilities, turning her universe into a bonfire of betrayal.

She finally realized why the wretch was so zealously guarding his identity.

Raja could literally see her doing the mental maths and reaching the obvious conclusion. He waited with bated breath—would her reaction be cataclysmic?

Dita could feel the anger simmering in her soul as she watched a smug grin appear on Palash's face. Between the father and the son, they had definitely managed to put her in a spot.

She turned towards Chirag, having made up her mind on the way she wanted to play this game. 'If the nation actually has any interest in knowing me, then let me introduce myself. I am Dita Roy, officiating principal of Phulpukur College. The love of my life is literature and I have little or no interest in any kind of sport or even in board games such as chess. I had no idea until now about the existence of Anuraj Bose, I only knew him as Raja, the boy who had once served me tea.'

The implied sting in her reply managed to stupefy and silence the ever-verbose Chirag.

Totally unable to control himself, Bob hollered with laughter, 'She just reduced chess to a board game, and an international champion to a tea boy!'

Chirag appeared miffed, 'But do you want to marry him or not?'

'Do you think my wants and desires are being taken into consideration here?' Dita pointed at Palash's gun. 'Father and son are equally duplicitous. Being a chess prodigy does not solve inherent problems! The sins of the father and the lies of the son!'

Palash frowned. Was Dita implying that Raja had lied to her? But when and why and how? His chain of thought was rudely broken by the harshest of words.

'And the answer to your question is no! No! I do not want to marry him.' Dita's vehement reaction echoed across the room.

Pom's heart went out to Raja, the poor boy looked crestfallen. At the same time, he could not step up to convince Dita because that would alert Palash to the actual dynamics of the Raja–Dita relationship. He found himself praying that Dita did not reveal the fact that she knew Raja only too well.

Dita's bold response had managed to wipe the smug smile off Palash's face. Infuriated beyond belief to be labelled as deceitful, he charged in like an angry bull, shoved Chirag aside, and pushed Dita back to the mandap. 'Your opinions are of no importance! Let's get this show on the road now,' he hissed, levelling the gun at her.

Girish barked out an order to Naveen Mukherjee and the rituals began. Trying to make the process easier, Naveen played out the holy mantras on his phone, which had been returned to him on Palash's orders; a visibly angry young woman, stiff with disapproval, and a much-troubled young man were made to sit in front of the holy fire to begin a chain of vows and promises.

Chirag continued to film the marriage proceedings right under the noses of Palash and Girish. Bob's men were recording too, covering every possible angle of the chaotic drama.

'It almost looks like a high-profile marriage; look at the media attention it is getting,' Papu muttered to Pinku and Sahana, as Dita and Raja stood up to take the prescribed seven pheras around the fire. 'She looks angry enough to kick Raja into the fire,' Sahana mumbled. 'This is not going to end well.'

Throughout the ceremony Raja could not take his eyes off Dita, burning bright and luminous with anger as she was, he felt himself drawn to her like a moth drawn to a flame. Here was a girl who could challenge the whole world to fight for what she thought was right; somehow, he would have to win her back, even if he had to travel to the end of the world to do so. Yet, uncertainty ruled. He felt an undertow of panic in his heart, for when he looked at her again, her eyes conveyed in no uncertain terms that he would remain unforgiven till the crack of doom. This is a marriage of heaven and hell, he mused, and right now, he was in purgatory.

Palash chortled with unholy glee: it would be impossible to find a more miserable bride and groom than the ones before his eyes. Serves them right for defying him at every turn, contravening well-laid plans. He sat down to enjoy the rest of the ceremony, making mental notes as to how he would stage a similar coup with Pom and Mishti.

Hemlata and Tamali watched the ceremony with apprehension, both of them knew that marrying off their offspring under such duress would not really resolve any issues. It was the menace of the guns that kept them silent; they could not rely on the whimsies of Palash or Girish! Neither Dita nor Raja were pliable characters, and what Palash had achieved here was just a temporary victory. Hemlata could not even imagine what she would do in case of a face-off between father and son after the wedding. She glanced at Pom, standing on the other side of the mandap, a look of silent appeal etched on her face; Pom looked up to catch her eye, the look of utter panic on his mother's face nearly tore his heart apart.

Raja noted the startled expression on Pom's face and looked back at his mother, trying to reassure her silently. He must have stopped moving for a second, for Dita, who was following him blindly on the rounds around the fire careened straight into him, stumbling and falling. The day's exhaustion was finally catching up—the hopelessness of the situation, the angst of betrayal, the frustration of losing faith escalated into a moment of sheer defeat; Dita literally felt the burden of the fight, the uncharacteristic bravado that she had imposed on herself, being crushed under the weight of dejection.

Sensing her falter, limp and listless, Raja reached out instinctively, catching her before she completely lost her balance, gravitating towards the flames in her haste to get away from him.

And then a strange thing happened: Raja bent down to pick Dita up, carrying her in his arms as they completed the last of the seven rounds around the fire. A hush descended on the crowd as they watched in disbelief the belligerent couple, who were thrown into the marriage as unwilling captives, morph into something totally unexpected. Raja's body language clearly radiated the concern and love he was experiencing for the frail girl ensconced in his embrace; all the fight seemed to have ebbed out of Dita as she instinctively melted into Raja's arms. She felt herself drowning once again in those grey eyes; the wretch was too handsome to resist, she realized, and far too caring!

Sensing the shift in her mood, Raja winked, as if to reassure her that no matter what, he was still that light-hearted boy whom she knew so well. Or did she? And even before she could gather a frown on that thought, Raja lowered his head to kiss her.

The crowd gasped! Pom cheered them on wildly! Pinku and Sahana broke out into a laugh of absolute joy and relief! And Chirag captured every priceless moment!

Palash could not believe his eyes and groaned this was inexplicable—beyond his dreams, even beyond his nightmares! The girl must know black magic or sorcery, I'll be damned!

All's Well That Ends Well

*I*ndia is a land of inconsistencies.

When the shotgun wedding hit the media, it erupted as a sensational piece of news, capturing the imagination of the populace, staying in the breaking news segment for weeks.

A preening Chirag could not stop gloating over the fact that he had successfully unmasked the identity of Anuraj Bose, that too at a shotgun wedding. As the wedding shot to fame, so too did Palash Bose—he became infamous overnight.

Being infamous, however, is better than being ignored. Palash Bose was rather startled to find that he had secured for himself the reputation of a top-notch villain, having terrorized his own son to marry a girl for all the wrong reasons.

The much maligned man rued the day he had set eyes on Dita Roy; depression overrode his ambitions, he was sure that he would lose the forthcoming elections with all the negative publicity he had garnered for himself. He could see himself toting a shotgun, streaming on millions of screens across the nation for days on end and he had no doubt that this was the end of his fledgling political career.

But then, India is a land of inconsistencies.

Palash Bose won a landslide victory. The people of Phulpukur and Diamond Harbour were apparently enjoying the media focus, many of them had been interviewed by news channels to provide different perspectives of the shotgun wedding and offer insights into the characters of Palash, Anuraj, and Dita.

Phulpukur College morphed into a tourist attraction with guided tours narrating the sequence of the infamous wedding. Palash had successfully launched Phulpukur into the consciousness of an entire nation, and so the villagers voted for him.

The popularity of the anti-hero transformed him into a hero; after all, the Indian political scenario isn't exactly renowned for the lily-white reputation of its politicians. Palash Bose thrived and blossomed, as Machiavellians do, for the end always justifies the means.

82727

Acknowledgements

When I sat down to write, I realized it was like sailing into uncharted waters on a rudderless ship, what with this being my first attempt to sublimate the intangible musings of my mind into tangible words. I certainly could not have done this without the unstinting support of Kishaloy Roychowdhury, my husband, who is the wind beneath my wings, and a voice of sanity in all my insane ventures.

It was my son, Alekhyo Roychowdhury, who read the very first draft of the novel; he said it was not bad, not bad at all! Coming from his age group this was a green signal to proceed, if there ever was one! I can't thank him enough for his patience and honest feedback.

I would like to thank my dear friends Brototi Dasgupta, Debanjan Dasgupta, Sounak Chakraborty, Shivalik K. Pathania, Sonia Gupta, and Rohan Ray for offering invaluable opinions, and reading through multiple drafts and helping me find a safe harbour.

Vaswati Samanta and Jayati Bose have been my pillars of support, keeping me emotionally grounded through the doubts and misgivings of the creative process.

Finally, I would like to thank Aleph Book Company— especially the editors there—whose help and guidance made the publication of my first novel a wonderful experience.